AGATHA CHRISTIE

*Classic
Mysteries*

POIROT
MISS MARPLE

This edition specially produced in 1996
for Puzzler Collection by arrangement with
HarperCollins*Publishers*
77–85 Fulham Palace Road,
Hammersmith, London W6 8JB

Adapted from Poirot Investigates,
first published by The Bodley Head Limited 1924,
Copyright © Agatha Christie 1924,
and Thirteen Problems,
first published by Collins 1932,
Copyright © Agatha Christie Mallowan 1932

ISBN 0 583 32621 8

Printed in Great Britain

CONTENTS

The Blue Geranium

'When I was down here last year – ' said Sir Henry Clithering, and stopped.

His hostess, Mrs Bantry, looked at him curiously.

The Ex-Commissioner of Scotland Yard was staying with old friends of his, Colonel and Mrs Bantry, who lived near St Mary Mead.

Mrs Bantry, pen in hand, had just asked his advice as to who should be invited to make a sixth guest at dinner that evening.

'Yes?' said Mrs Bantry encouragingly. 'When you were here last year?'

'Tell me,' said Sir Henry, 'do you know a Miss Marple?'

Mrs Bantry was surprised. It was the last thing she had expected.

'Know Miss Marple? Who doesn't! The typical old maid of fiction. Quite a dear, but hopelessly behind the times. Do you mean you would like me to ask *her* to dinner?'

'You are surprised?'

'A little, I must confess. I should hardly have thought you – but perhaps there's an explanation?'

'The explanation is simple enough. When I was down here last year we got into the habit of discussing unsolved mysteries – there were five or six of us – Raymond West, the novelist, started it. We each supplied a story to which we knew the answer, but nobody else did. It was supposed to be an exercise in the deductive faculties – to see who could get nearest the truth.'

'Well?'

'Like in the old story – we hardly realized that Miss Marple was playing; but we were very polite about it – didn't want to hurt the old dear's feelings. And now comes the cream of the jest. The old lady outdid us every time!'

'What?'

'I assure you – straight to the truth like a homing pigeon.'

'But how extraordinary! Why, dear old Miss Marple has hardly ever been out of St Mary Mead.'

'Ah! But according to her, that has given her unlimited opportunities of observing human nature – under the microscope as it were.'

'I suppose there's something in that,' conceded Mrs Bantry. 'One would at least know the petty side of people. But I don't think we have any really exciting criminals in our midst. I think we must try her with Arthur's ghost story after dinner. I'd be thankful if she'd find a solution to that.'

'I didn't know that Arthur believed in ghosts?'

'Oh! he doesn't. That's what worries him so. And it happened to a friend of his, George Pritchard – a most prosaic person. It's really rather tragic for poor George. Either this extraordinary story is true – or else –'

'Or else what?'

Mrs Bantry did not answer. After a minute or two she said irrelevantly:

'You know, I like George – everyone does. One can't believe that he – but people do do such extraordinary things.'

Sir Henry nodded. He knew, better than Mrs Bantry, the extraordinary things that people did.

So it came about that that evening Mrs Bantry looked round her dinner table (shivering a little as she did so, because the dining-room, like most English dining-rooms, was extremely cold) and fixed her gaze on the very upright old lady sitting on her husband's right. Miss Marple wore black lace mittens; an old lace fichu was draped round her shoulders and another piece of lace surmounted her white hair. She was talking animatedly to the elderly doctor, Dr Lloyd, about the Workhouse and the suspected shortcomings of the District Nurse.

Mrs Bantry marvelled anew. She even wondered whether Sir Henry had been making an elaborate joke – but there seemed no point in that. Incredible that what he had said could be really true.

Her glance went on and rested affectionately on her red-faced broad-shouldered husband as he sat talking horses to Jane Helier, the beautiful and popular actress. Jane, more beautiful (if that were possible) off the stage than on, opened enormous blue eyes and murmured at discreet intervals: "Really?" "Oh fancy!" "How extraordinary!" She knew nothing whatever about horses and cared less.

'Arthur,' said Mrs Bantry, 'you're boring poor Jane to distraction. Leave horses alone and tell her your ghost story instead. You know . . . George Pritchard.'

'Eh, Dolly? Oh! but I don't know –'

'Sir Henry wants to hear it too. I was telling him something about it this morning. It would be interesting to hear what everyone has to say about it.'

'Oh do!' said Jane. 'I love ghost stories.'

'Well –' Colonel Bantry hesitated. 'I've never believed much in the supernatural. But this –

'I don't think any of you know George Pritchard. He's one of the best. His wife – well, she's dead now, poor woman. I'll just say this much: she didn't give George any too easy a time when she was alive. She was one of those semi-invalids – I believe she had really something wrong with her, but whatever it was she played it for all it was worth. She was capricious, exacting, unreasonable. She complained from morning to night. George was expected to wait on her hand and foot, and every thing he did was always wrong and he got cursed for it. Most men, I'm fully convinced, would have hit her over the head with a hatchet long ago. Eh, Dolly, isn't that so?'

'She was a dreadful woman,' said Mrs Bantry with conviction. 'If George Pritchard had brained her with a hatchet, and there had been any woman on the jury, he would have been triumphantly acquitted.'

'I don't quite know how this business started. George was rather vague about it. I gather Mrs Pritchard had always had a weakness for fortune tellers, palmists, clairvoyantes – anything of that sort. George didn't mind. If she found amusement in it well and good. But he refused to go into rhapsodies himself, and that was another grievance.

'A succession of hospital nurses was always passing through the house, Mrs Pritchard usually becoming dissatisfied with them after a few weeks. One young nurse had been very keen on this fortune telling stunt, and for a time Mrs Pritchard had been very fond of her. Then she suddenly fell out with her and insisted on her going. She had back another nurse who had been with her previously – an older woman, experienced and tactful in dealing with a neurotic patient. Nurse Copling, according to George, was a very good sort – a sensible woman to talk to. She put up with Mrs Pritchard's tantrums and nervestorms with complete indifference.

'Mrs Pritchard always lunched upstairs, and it was usual at lunch time for George and the nurse to come to some arrangement for the afternoon. Strictly speaking, the nurse went off from two to four, but "to oblige" as the phrase goes, she would sometimes take her time off after tea if George wanted to be free for the afternoon. On this occasion, she mentioned that she was going to see a sister at Golders Green and might be a little late returning. George's face fell, for he had arranged to play a round of golf. Nurse Copling, however, reassured him.

'"We'll neither of us be missed, Mr Pritchard." A twinkle

came into her eye. "Mrs Pritchard's going to have more exciting company than ours."

'"Who's that?"

'"Wait a minute," Nurse Copling's eyes twinkled more than ever. "Let me get it right. *Zarida, Psychic Reader of the Future.*"

'"Oh Lord!" groaned George. "That's a new one, isn't it?"

'"Quite new. I believe my predecessor, Nurse Carstairs, sent her along. Mrs Pritchard hasn't seen her yet. She made me write, fixing an appointment for this afternoon."

'"Well, at any rate, I shall get my golf," said George, and he went off with the kindliest feelings towards Zarida, the Reader of the Future.

'On his return to the house, he found Mrs Pritchard in a state of great agitation. She was, as usual, lying on her invalid couch, and she had a bottle of smelling salts in her hand which she sniffed at frequent intervals.

'"George," she exclaimed. "What did I tell you about this house? The moment I came into it, I *felt* there was something wrong! Didn't I tell you so at the time?"

'Repressing his desire to reply, "You always do," George said, "No, I can't say I remember it."

'"You never do remember anything that has to do with me. Men are all extraordinarily callous – but I really believe that you are even more insensitive than most."

'"Oh, come now, Mary dear, that's not fair."

'"Well, as I was telling you, this woman *knew* at once! She – she actually blenched – if you know what I mean – as she came in at the door, and she said: 'There is evil here – evil and danger. I feel it.'"'

'Very unwisely George laughed.

'"Well, you have had your money's worth this afternoon."

'His wife closed her eyes and took a long sniff from her smelling bottle.

'"How you hate me! You would jeer and laugh if I were dying."

'George protested and after a minute or two she went on.

'"You may laugh, but I shall tell you the whole thing. This house is definitely dangerous to me – the woman said so."

'George's formerly kind feeling towards Zarida underwent a change. He knew his wife was perfectly capable of insisting on moving to a new house if the caprice got hold of her.

'"What else did she say?" he asked.

'"She couldn't tell me very much. She was so upset. One thing she did say. I had some violets in a glass. She pointed at them and cried out:

'"Take those away. No blue flowers – never have blue flowers. *Blue flowers are fatal to you – remember that.*"'

'"And you know," added Mrs Pritchard, "I always have told you that blue as a colour is repellent to me. I feel a natural instinctive sort of warning against."

'George was much too wise to remark that he had never heard her say so before. Instead he asked what the mysterious Zarida was like. Mrs Pritchard entered with gusto upon a description.

'"Black hair in coiled knobs over her ears – her eyes were half closed – great black rims round them – she had a black veil over her mouth and chin – and she spoke in a kind of singing voice with a marked foreign accent – Spanish, I think –"

'"In fact all the usual stock-in-trade," said George cheerfully.

'His wife immediately closed her eyes.

'"I feel extremely ill," she said. "Ring for nurse. Unkindness upsets me, as you know only too well."

'It was two days later that Nurse Copling came to George with a grave face.

'"Will you come to Mrs Pritchard, please. She has had a letter which upsets her greatly."

'He found his wife with the letter in her hand. She held it out to him.

'"Read it," she said.

'George read it. It was on heavily scented paper, and the writing was big and black.

'*I have seen the future. Be warned before it is too late. Beware of the Full Moon. The Blue Primrose means Warning; the Blue Hollyhock means Danger; the Blue Geranium means Death . . .*

'Just about to burst out laughing, George caught Nurse Copling's eye. She made a quick warning gesture. He said rather awkwardly, "The woman's probably trying to frighten you, Mary. Anyway there aren't such things as blue primroses and blue geraniums."

'But Mrs Pritchard began to cry and say her days were numbered. Nurse Copling came out with George upon the landing.

'"Of all the silly tomfoolery," he burst out.

'"I suppose it is."

'Something in the nurse's tone struck him, and he stared at her in amazement.

'"Surely, nurse, you don't believe – "

'"No, no, Mr Pritchard. I don't believe in reading the future – that's nonsense. What puzzles me is the *meaning* of this. Fortune-tellers are usually out for what they can get. But this woman seems to be frightening Mrs Pritchard with no advantage to herself. I can't see the point. There's another thing – "

'"Yes?"

'"Mrs Pritchard says that something about Zarida was faintly familiar to her."

'"Well?"

'"Well, I don't like it, Mr Pritchard, that's all."

'"I didn't know you were so superstitious, nurse."

'"I'm not superstitious; but I know when a thing is fishy."

'It was about four days after this that the first incident happened. To explain it to you, I shall have to describe Mrs Pritchard's room –'

'You'd better let me do that,' interrupted Mrs Bantry. 'It was papered with one of those new wallpapers where you apply clumps of flowers to make a kind of herbaceous border. The effect is almost like being in a garden – though, of course, the flowers are all wrong. I mean they simply couldn't be in bloom all at the same time –'

'Don't let a passion for horticultural accuracy run away with you, Dolly,' said her husband. 'We all know you're an enthusiastic gardener.'

'Well, it *is* absurd,' protested Mrs Bantry. 'To have bluebells and daffodils and lupins and hollyhocks and Michaelmas daisies all grouped together.'

'Most unscientific,' said Sir Henry. 'But to proceed with the story.'

'Well, among these massed flowers were primroses, clumps of yellow and pink primroses and – oh go on, Arthur, this is your story –'

Colonel Bantry took up the tale.

'Mrs Pritchard rang her bell violently one morning. The household came running – thought she was in extremis; not at all. She was violently excited and pointing at the wallpaper; and there sure enough was *one blue primrose* in the midst of the others . . .'

'Oh!' said Miss Helier, 'how creepy!'

'The question was: Hadn't the blue primrose always been there? That was George's suggestion and the nurse's. But Mrs Pritchard wouldn't have it at any price. She had never noticed it till that very morning and the night before had been full moon. She was very upset about it.'

'I met George Pritchard that same day and he told me about it,' said Mrs Bantry. 'I went to see Mrs Pritchard and did my best to ridicule the whole thing; but without success. I came away really concerned, and I remember I met Jean Instow and told her about it. Jean is a queer girl. She said, "So she's really upset about it?" I told her that I thought the woman was perfectly capable of dying of fright – she was really abnormally superstitious.

'I remember Jean rather startled me with what she said next. She said, "Well, that might be all for the best, mightn't it?" And she said it so coolly, in so matter-of-fact a tone that I was really – well, shocked. Of course I know it's done nowadays – to be brutal and outspoken; but I never get used to it. Jean smiled at me rather oddly and said, "You don't like my saying that – but it's true. What use is Mrs Pritchard's life to her? None at all; and it's hell for George Pritchard. To have his wife frightened out of existence would be the best thing that could happen to him." I said, "George is most awfully good to her always." And she said, "Yes, he deserves a reward, poor dear. He's a very attractive person, George ·Pritchard. The last nurse thought so – the pretty one – what was her name? Carstairs. That was the cause of the row between her and Mrs P."

'Now I didn't like hearing Jean say that. Of course one had *wondered* –'

Mrs Bantry paused significantly.

'Yes, dear,' said Miss Marple placidly. 'One always does. Is Miss Instow a pretty girl? I suppose she plays golf?'

'Yes. She's good at all games. And she's nice looking, attractive-looking, very fair with a healthy skin, and nice steady blue eyes. Of course we always have felt that she and George Pritchard – I mean if things had been different – they are so well suited to one another.'

'And they were friends?' asked Miss Marple.

'Oh yes. Great friends.'

'Do you think, Dolly,' said Colonel Bantry plaintively, 'that I might be allowed to go on with my story?'

'Arthur,' said Mrs Bantry resignedly, 'wants to get back to his ghosts.'

'I had the rest of the story from George himself,' went on the colonel. 'There's no doubt that Mrs Pritchard got the wind up badly towards the end of the next month. She marked off on a calendar the day when the moon would be full, and on that night she had both the nurse and then George into her room and made them study the wallpaper carefully. There were pink hollyhocks and red ones, but there were no blue amongst them. Then when George left the room she locked the door –'

'And in the morning there was a large blue hollyhock,' said Miss Helier joyfully.

'Quite right,' said Colonel Bantry. 'Or at any rate, nearly right. One flower of a hollyhock just above her head had turned blue. It staggered George; and of course the more it staggered him the more he refused to take the thing seriously. He insisted that the whole thing was some kind of practical joke. He ignored the evidence of the locked door and the fact that Mrs Pritchard discovered the change before anyone – even Nurse Copling – was admitted.

'It staggered George; and it made him unreasonable. His wife wanted to leave the house, and he wouldn't let her. He was inclined to believe in the supernatural for the first time, but he wasn't going to admit it. He usually gave in to his wife, but this time he wouldn't. Mary was not to make a fool of herself, he said. The whole thing was the most infernal nonsense.

'And so the next month sped away. Mrs Pritchard made less protest than one would have imagined. I think she was superstitious enough to believe that she couldn't escape her fate. She repeated again and again: "The blue primrose – warning. The blue hollyhock – danger. The blue geranium – *death*." And she would lie looking at the clump of pinky-red geraniums nearest her bed.

'The whole business was pretty nervy. Even the nurse caught the infection. She came to George two days before full moon and begged him to take Mrs Pritchard away. George was angry.

'"If all the flowers on that damned wall turned into blue devils it couldn't kill anyone!" he shouted.

'"It might. Shock has killed people before now."

'"Nonsense," said George.

George has always been a shade pig-headed. You can't drive him. I believe he had a secret idea that his wife worked the changed herself and that it was all some morbid hysterical plan of hers.

'Well, the fatal night came. Mrs Pritchard locked the door as usual. She was very calm – in almost an exalted state of mind. The nurse was worried by her state – wanted to give her a stimulant, an injection of strychnine, but Mrs Pritchard refused. In a way, I believe, she was enjoying herself. George said she was.'

'I think that's quite possible,' said Mrs Bantry. 'There must have been a strange sort of glamour about the whole thing.'

'There was no violent ringing of a bell the next morning. Mrs Pritchard usually woke about eight. When, at eight-thirty, there was no sign from her, nurse rapped loudly on the door. Getting no reply, she fetched George, and insisted on the door being broken open. They did so with the help of a chisel.

'One look at the still figure on the bed was enough for Nurse Copling. She sent George to telephone for the doctor, but it was too late. Mrs Pritchard, he said, must have been dead at least eight hours. Her smelling salts lay by her hand on the bed, *and on the wall beside her one of the pinky-red geraniums was a bright deep blue*.'

'Horrible,' said Miss Helier with a shiver.

Sir Henry was frowning.

'No additional details?'

Colonel Bantry shook his head, but Mrs Bantry spoke quickly.

'The gas.'

'What about the gas?' asked Sir Henry.

'When the doctor arrived there was a slight smell of gas, and sure enough he found the gas ring in the fireplace very slightly turned on; but so little it couldn't have mattered.'

'Did Mr Pritchard and the nurse not notice it when they first went in?'

'The nurse said she did notice a slight smell. George said he didn't notice gas, but something made him feel very queer and overcome; but he put that down to shock – and probably it was. At any rate there was no question of gas poisoning. The smell was scarcely noticeable.'

'And that's the end of the story?'

'No, it isn't. One way and another, there was a lot of talk. The servants, you see, had overheard things – had heard, for instance, Mrs Pritchard telling her husband that he hated her and would jeer if she were dying. And also more recent remarks. She had said one day, apropos of his refusing to leave the house: "Very well, when I am dead, I hope everyone will realize that you have killed me." And as ill luck would have it, he had been mixing some weed killer for the garden paths the day before. One of the younger servants had seen him and had afterwards seen him taking up a glass of hot milk for his wife.

'The talk spread and grew. The doctor had given a certificate – I don't know exactly in what terms – shock, syncope, heart failure, probably some medical terms meaning nothing much. However the poor lady had not been a month in her grave before an exhumation order was applied for and granted.'

'And the result of the autopsy was nil, I remember,' said

Sir Henry gravely. 'A case, for once, of smoke without fire.'

'The whole thing is really very curious,' said Mrs Bantry. 'That fortune-teller, for instance – Zarida. At the address where she was supposed to be, no one had ever heard of any such person!'

'She appeared once – out of the blue,' said her husband, 'and then utterly vanished. Out of the *blue* – that's rather good!'

'And what is more,' continued Mrs Bantry, 'little Nurse Carstairs, who was supposed to have recommended her, had never even heard of her.'

They looked at each other.

'It's a mysterious story,' said Dr Lloyd. 'One can make guesses; but to guess –'

He shook his head.

'Has Mr Pritchard married Miss Instow?' asked Miss Marple in her gentle voice.

'Now why do you ask that?' inquired Sir Henry.

Miss Marple opened gentle blue eyes.

'It seems to me so important,' she said. 'Have they married?'

Colonel Bantry shook his head.

'We – well, we expected something of the kind – but it's eighteen months now. I don't believe they even see much of each other.'

'That is important,' said Miss Marple. 'Very important.'

'Then you think the same as I do,' said Mrs Bantry. 'You think –'

'Now, Dolly,' said her husband. 'It's unjustifiable – what you're going to say. You can't go about accusing people without a shadow of proof.'

'Don't be so – so manly, Arthur. Men are always afraid to say *anything*. Anyway, this is all between ourselves. It's just a wild fantastic idea of mine that possibly – only *possibly* – Jean Instow disguised herself as a fortune-teller. Mind you, she may have done it for a joke. I don't for a minute think that she meant any harm; but if she did do it, and if Mrs Pritchard was foolish enough to die of fright – well, that's what Miss Marple meant, wasn't it?'

'No, dear, not quite,' said Miss Marple. 'You see, if I were going to kill anyone – which, of course, I wouldn't dream of doing for a minute, because it would be very wicked, and besides I don't like killing – not even wasps, though I know it has to be, and I'm sure the gardener does it as humanely as possible. Let me see, what was I saying?'

'If you wished to kill anyone,' prompted Sir Henry.

'Oh yes. Well, if I did, I shouldn't be at all satisfied to trust to *fright*. I know one reads of people dying of it, but it seems a very uncertain sort of thing, and the most nervous people are far more brave than one really thinks they are. I should like something definite and certain, and make a thoroughly good plan about it.'

'Miss Marple,' said Sir Henry, 'you frighten me. I hope you will never wish to remove me. Your plans would be too good.'

Miss Marple looked at him reproachfully.

'I thought I had made it clear that I would never contemplate such wickedness,' she said. 'No, I was trying to put myself in the place of – er – a certain person.'

'Do you mean George Pritchard?' asked Colonel Bantry. 'I'll never believe it of George – though – mind you, even the nurse believes it. I went and saw her about a month afterwards, at the time of the exhumation. She didn't know how it was done – in fact, she wouldn't say anything at all – but it was clear enough that she believed George to be in some way responsible for his wife's death. She was convinced of it.'

'Well,' said Dr Lloyd, 'perhaps she wasn't so far wrong. And mind you, a nurse often *knows*. She can't say – she's got no proof – but she *knows*.'

Sir Henry leant forward.

'Come now, Miss Marple,' he said persuasively.

'You're lost in a daydream. Won't you tell us all about it?'

Miss Marple started and turned pink.

'I beg your pardon,' she said. 'I was just thinking about our District Nurse. A most difficult problem.'

'More difficult than the problem of the blue geranium?'

'It really depends on the primroses,' said Miss Marple. 'I mean, Mrs Bantry said they were yellow and pink. If it was a pink primrose that turned blue, of course, that fits in perfectly. But if it happened to be a yellow one –'

'It was a pink one,' said Mrs Bantry.

She stared. They all stared at Miss Marple.

'Then that seems to settle it,' said Miss Marple. She shook her head regretfully. 'And the wasp season and everything. And of course the gas.'

'It reminds you, I suppose, of countless village tragedies?' said Sir Henry.

'Not tragedies,' said Miss Marple. 'And certainly nothing criminal. But it does remind me a little of the trouble we are having with the District Nurse. After all, nurses are human beings, and what with having to be so correct in their behaviour and wearing those uncomfortable collars and being so thrown with the family – well, can you wonder that things sometimes happen?'

A glimmer of light broke upon Sir Henry.

'You mean Nurse Carstairs?'

'Oh no. Not Nurse Carstairs. Nurse *Copling*. You see, she had been there before, and very much thrown with Mr Pritchard, who you say is an attractive man. I daresay she thought, poor thing – well, we needn't go into that. I don't suppose she knew about Miss Instow, and of course afterwards, when she found out, it turned her against him and she tried to do all the harm she could. Of course the letter really gave her away, didn't it?'

'What letter?'

'Well, she wrote to the fortune-teller at Mrs Pritchard's request, and the fortune-teller came, apparently in answer to the letter. But later it was discovered that there never had been such a person at that address. So that shows that Nurse Copling was in it. She only pretended to write – so what could be more likely than that *she* was the fortune teller herself?'

'I never saw the point about the letter,' said Sir Henry. 'That's a most important point, of course.'

'Rather a bold step to take,' said Miss Marple, 'because Mrs Pritchard might have recognized her in spite of the disguise – though of course if she had, the nurse could have pretended it was a joke.'

'What did you mean,' said Sir Henry, 'when you said that if you were a certain person you would not have trusted to fright?'

'One couldn't be *sure* that way,' said Miss Marple. 'No, I think that the warnings and the blue flowers were, if I may use a military term,' she laughed self-consciously – '*just camouflage.*'

'And the real thing?'

'I know,' said Miss Marple apologetically, 'that I've got wasps on the brain. Poor things, destroyed in their thousands – and usually on such a beautiful summer's day. But I remember thinking, when I saw the gardener shaking up the cyanide of potassium in a bottle with water, how like smelling-salts it looked. And if it were put in a smelling-salt bottle and substituted for the real one – well, the poor lady was in the habit of using her smelling-salts. Indeed you said they were found by her hand. Then, of course, while Mr Pritchard went to telephone to the doctor, the nurse would change it for the real bottle, and she'd just turn on the gas a little bit to mask any smell of almonds and in case anyone felt queer, and I always have heard that cyanide leaves no trace if you wait long enough. But, of course I may be wrong, and it may have been something entirely different in the bottle; but that doesn't really matter, does it?'

Miss Marple paused, a little out of breath.

Jane Helier leant forward and said, 'But the blue geranium, and the other flowers?'

'Nurses always have litmus paper, don't they?' said Miss Marple, 'for – well, for testing. Not a very pleasant subject. We won't dwell on it. I have done a little nursing myself.' She grew delicately pink. 'Blue turns red with acids, and red turns blue with alkalis. So easy to paste some red litmus over a red flower – near the bed, of course. And then, when the poor lady used her smelling-salts, the strong ammonia fumes would turn it blue. Really most ingenious. Of course, the geranium wasn't blue when they first broke into the room – nobody noticed it till afterwards. When nurse changed the bottles, she held the Sal Ammoniac against the wallpaper for a minute, I expect.'

'You might have been there, Miss Marple,' said Sir Henry.

'What worries me,' said Miss Marple, 'is poor Mr Pritchard and that nice girl, Miss Instow. Probably both suspecting each other and keeping apart – and life so very short.'

She shook her head.

'You needn't worry,' said Sir Henry. 'As a matter of fact I have something up my sleeve. A nurse has been arrested on a charge of murdering an elderly patient who had left her a legacy. It was done with cyanide of potassium substituted for smelling-salts. Nurse Copling trying the same trick again. Miss Instow and Mr Pritchard need have no doubts as to the truth.'

'Now isn't that nice?' cried Miss Marple. 'I don't mean about the new murder, of course. That's very sad, and shows how much wickedness there is in the world, and that if once you give way – which reminds me I *must* finish my little conversation with Dr Lloyd about the village nurse.'

The Four Suspects

The conversation hovered round undiscovered and unpunished crimes. Everyone in turn vouchsafed their opinion: Colonel Bantry, his plump amiable wife, Jane Helier, Dr Lloyd, and even old Miss Marple. The one person who did not speak was the one best fitted in most people's opinion to do so. Sir Henry Clithering, ex-Commissioner of Scotland Yard, sat silent, twisting his moustache – or rather stroking it – and half smiling, as though at some inward thought that amused him.

'Sir Henry,' said Mrs Bantry at last. 'If you don't say something I shall scream. Are there a lot of crimes that go unpunished, or are there not?'

'You're thinking of newspaper headlines, Mrs Bantry. SCOTLAND YARD AT FAULT AGAIN. And a list of unsolved mysteries to follow.'

'Which really, I suppose, form a very small percentage of the whole?' said Dr Lloyd.

'Yes; that is so. The hundreds of crimes that are solved and the perpetrators punished are seldom heralded and sung. But that isn't quite the point at issue, is it? When you talk of *undiscovered* crimes and *unsolved* crimes, you are talking of two different things. In the first category come all the crimes that Scotland Yard never hears about, the crimes that no one even knows have been committed.'

'But I suppose there aren't very many of those?' said Mrs Bantry.

'Aren't there?'

'Sir Henry! You don't mean there *are*?'

'I should think,' said Miss Marple thoughtfully, 'that there must be a very large number.'

The charming old lady, with her old-world unruffled air, made her statement in a tone of the utmost placidity.

'My dear Miss Marple,' said Colonel Bantry.

'Of course,' said Miss Marple, 'a lot of people are stupid. And stupid people get found out, whatever they do. But there are quite a number of people who aren't stupid, and one shudders to think of what they might accomplish unless they had very strongly rooted principles.'

'Yes,' said Sir Henry, 'there are a lot of people who aren't stupid. How often does some crime come to light simply by reason of a bit of unmitigated bungling, and each time one asks oneself the question: If this hadn't been bungled, would anyone ever have known?'

'But that's very serious, Clithering,' said Colonel Bantry. 'Very serious, indeed.'

'Is it?'

'What do you mean! It is! Of course it's serious.'

'You say crime goes unpunished; but does it? Unpunished by the law perhaps; but cause and effect works outside the law. To say that every crime brings its own punishment is by way of being a platitude, and yet in my opinion nothing can be truer.'

'Perhaps, perhaps,' said Colonel Bantry. 'But that doesn't alter the seriousness – the – er – seriousness –' He paused, rather at a loss.

Sir Henry Clithering smiled.

'Ninety-nine people out of a hundred are doubtless of your way of thinking,' he said. 'But you know, it isn't really guilt that is important – it's innocence. That's the thing that nobody will realize.'

'I don't understand,' said Jane Helier.

'I do,' said Miss Marple. 'When Mrs Trent found half a crown missing from her bag, the person it affected most was the daily woman, Mrs Arthur. Of course the Trents thought it was her, but being kindly people and knowing she had a large family and a husband who drinks, well – they naturally didn't want to go to extremes. But they felt differently towards her, and they didn't leave her in charge of the house when they went away, which made a great difference to her; and other people began to get a feeling about her too. And then it suddenly came out that it was the governess. Mrs Trent saw her through a door reflected in a mirror. The purest chance – though I prefer to call it Providence. And that, I think, is what Sir Henry means. Most people would be only interested in who took the money, and it turned out to be the most unlikely person – just like in detective stories! But the real person it was life and death to was poor Mrs Arthur, who had done nothing. That's what you mean, isn't it, Sir Henry?'

'Yes, Miss Marple, you've hit off my meaning exactly. Your charwoman person was lucky in the instance you relate. Her innocence was shown. But some people may go through a lifetime crushed by the weight of a suspicion that is really unjustified.'

'Are you thinking of some particular instance, Sir Henry?' asked Mrs Bantry shrewdly.

'As a matter of fact, Mrs Bantry, I am. A very curious case. A case where we believe murder to have been committed, but with no possible chance of ever proving it.'

'Poison, I suppose,' breathed Jane. 'Something untraceable.'

Dr Lloyd moved restlessly and Sir Henry shook his head.

'No, dear lady. *Not* the secret arrow poison of the South American Indians! I wish it *were* something of that kind. We have to deal with something much more prosaic – so prosaic, in fact, that there is no hope of bringing the deed home to its perpetrator. An old gentleman who fell downstairs and broke his neck; one of those regrettable accidents which happen every day.'

'But what happened really?'

'Who can say?' Sir Henry shrugged his shoulders. 'A push from behind? A piece of cotton or string tied across the top of the stairs and carefully removed afterwards? That we shall never know.'

'But you do think that it – well, wasn't an accident? Now why?' asked the doctor.

'That's rather a long story, but – well, yes, we're pretty sure. As I said there's no chance of being able to bring the deed home to anyone – the evidence would be too flimsy. But there's the other aspect of the case – the one I was speaking about. You see, there were four people who might have done the trick. One's guilty; *but the other three are innocent.* And unless the truth is found out, those three are going to remain under the terrible shadow of doubt.'

'I think,' said Mrs Bantry, 'that you'd better tell us your long story.'

'I needn't make it so very long after all,' said Sir Henry. 'I can at any rate condense the beginning. That deals with a German secret society – the Schwartze Hand – something after the lines of the Camorra or what is most people's idea of the Camorra. A scheme of blackmail and terrorization. The thing started quite suddenly after the War, and spread to an amazing extent. Numberless people were victimized by it. The authorities were not successful in coping with it, for its secrets were jealously guarded, and it was almost impossible to find anyone who could be induced to betray them.

'Nothing much was ever known about it in England, but in Germany it was having a most paralysing effect. It was finally broken up and dispersed through the efforts of one man, a Dr Rosen, who had at one time been very prominent in Secret Service work. He became a member, penetrated its inmost circle, and was, as I say, instrumental in bringing about its downfall.

'But he was, in consequence, a marked man, and it was deemed wise that he should leave Germany – at any rate for a time. He came to England, and we had letters about him from the police in Berlin. He came and had a personal interview with me. His point of view was both dispassionate and resigned. He had no doubts of what the future held for him.

'"They will get me, Sir Henry," he said. "Not a doubt of it." He was a big man with a fine head, and a very deep voice, with only a slight guttural intonation to tell of his nationality. "That is a foregone conclusion. It does not matter, I am prepared. I faced the risk when I undertook this business. I have done what I set out to do. The organization can never be got together again. But there are many members of it at liberty, and they will take the only revenge they can – my life. It is simply a question of time; but I am anxious that that time should be as long as possible. You see, I am collecting and editing some very interesting material – the result of my life's work. I should like, if possible, to be able to complete my task."

'He spoke very simply, with a certain grandeur which I could not but admire. I told him we would take all precautions, but he waved my words aside.

'"Some day, sooner or later, they will get me," he repeated. "When that day comes, do not distress yourself. You will, I have no doubt, have done all that is possible."

'He then proceeded to outline his plans which were simple enough. He proposed to take a small cottage in the country where he could live quietly and go on with his work. In the end he selected a village in Somerset – King's Gnaton, which was seven miles from a railway station, and singularly untouched by civilization. He bought a very charming cottage, had various improvements and alterations made, and settled down there most contentedly. His household consisted of his niece, Greta, a secretary, an old German servant who had served him faithfully for nearly forty years, and an outside handyman and gardener who was a native of King's Gnaton.'

'The four suspects,' said Dr Lloyd softly.

'Exactly. The four suspects. There is not much more to tell. Life went on peacefully at King's Gnaton for five months and then the blow fell. Dr Rosen fell down the stairs one morning and was found dead about half an hour later. At the time the accident must have taken place, Gertrud was in her kitchen with the door closed and heard nothing – so *she* says. Fräulein Greta was in the garden planting some bulbs – again, so *she* says. The gardener, Dobbs, was in the small potting shed having his elevenses – so *he* says; and the secretary was out for a walk, and once more there is only his own word for it. No one has an alibi – no one can corroborate anyone else's story. But one thing *is* certain. No one from outside could have done it, for a stranger in the little village of King's Gnaton would be noticed without fail. Both the back and the front doors were locked, each member of the household having their own key. So you see it narrows down to those four. And yet each one seems to be above suspicion. Greta, his own brother's child. Gertrud, with forty years of faithful service. Dobbs, who has never been out of King's Gnaton. And Charles Templeton, the secretary –'

'Yes,' said Colonel Bantry, 'what about him? He seems the suspicious person to my mind. What do you know about him?'

'It is what I knew about him that put him completely out of court – at any rate at the time,' said Sir Henry gravely. 'You see, Charles Templeton was one of my own men.'

'Oh!' said Colonel Bantry, considerably taken aback.

'Yes. I wanted to have someone on the spot, and at the same time I didn't want to cause talk in the village. Rosen really needed a secretary. I put Templeton on the job. He's a gentleman, he speaks German fluently, and he's altogether a very able fellow.'

'But, then, which do you suspect?' asked Mrs Bantry in a bewildered tone. 'They all seem so – well, impossible.'

'Yes, so it appears. But you can look at the thing from another angle. Fräulein Greta was his niece and a very lovely girl, but the War has shown us time and again that brother can turn against sister, or father against son and so on, and the loveliest and gentlest of young girls did some of the most amazing things. The same thing applies to Gertrud, and who knows what other forces might be at work in her case. A quarrel, perhaps, with her master, a growing resentment all the more lasting because of the long faithful years behind her. Elderly women of that class can be amazingly bitter sometimes. And Dobbs? Was he right outside it because he had no connection with the family? Money will do much. In some way Dobbs might have been approached and bought.

'For one thing seems certain: Some message or some order must have come from outside. Otherwise why five months immunity? No, the agents of the society must have been at work. Not yet sure of Rosen's perfidy, they delayed till the betrayal had been traced to him beyond any possible doubt. And then, all doubts set aside, they must have sent their message to the spy within the gates – the message that said, "Kill".'

'How nasty!' said Jane Helier, and shuddered.

'But how did the message come? That was the point I tried to elucidate – the one hope of solving my problem. One of those four people must have been approached or communicated with in some way. There would be no delay – I knew that – as soon as the command came, it would be carried out. That was a peculiarity of the Schwartze Hand.

'I went into the question, went into it in a way that will probably strike you as being ridiculously meticulous. Who had come to the cottage that morning? I eliminated nobody. Here is the list.'

He took an envelope from his pocket and selected a paper from its contents.

'*The butcher*, bringing some neck of mutton. Investigated and found correct.

'*The grocer's assistant*, bringing a packet of cornflour, two pounds of sugar, a pound of butter, and a pound of coffee. Also investigated and found correct.

'*The postman*, bringing two circulars for Fräulein Rosen, a local letter for Gertrud, three letters for Dr Rosen, one with a foreign stamp and two letters for Mr Templeton, one also with a foreign stamp.'

Sir Henry paused and then took a sheaf of documents from the envelope.

'It may interest you to see these for yourself. They were handed me by the various people concerned, or collected from the waste-paper basket. I need hardly say they've been tested by experts for invisible ink, etc. No excitement of that kind is possible.'

Everyone crowded round to look. The catalogues were respectively from a nurseryman and from a prominent London fur establishment. The two bills addressed to Dr Rosen were a local one for seeds for the garden and one from a London stationery firm. The letter addressed to him ran as follows:

My Dear Rosen – Just back from Dr Helmuth Spath's. I saw Edgar Jackson the other day. He and Amos Perry have just come back from Tsingtau. In all Honesty I can't say I envy them the trip. Let me have news of you soon. As I said before: Beware of a certain person. You know who I mean, though you don't agree. – Yours, Georgine.

'Mr Templeton's mail consisted of this bill, which as you see, is an account rendered from his tailor, and a letter from a friend in Germany,' went on Sir Henry. 'The latter, unfortunately, he tore up whilst out on his walk. Finally we have the letter received by Gertrud.'

> Dear Mrs Swartz, — We're hoping as how you be able to come the social on friday evening, the vicar says has he hopes you will — one and all being welcome. The resipy for the ham was very good, and I thanks you for it. Hoping as this finds you well and that we shall see you friday I remain. — Yours faithfully, Emma Greene.

Dr Lloyd smiled a little over this and so did Mrs Bantry.

'I think the last letter can be put out of court,' said Dr Lloyd.

'I thought the same,' said Sir Henry; 'but I took the precaution of verifying that there was a Mrs Greene and a Church Social. One can't be too careful, you know.'

'That's what our friend Miss Marple always says,' said Dr Lloyd, smiling. 'You're lost in a daydream, Miss Marple. What are you thinking out?'

Miss Marple gave a start.

'So stupid of me,' she said. 'I was just wondering why the word Honesty in Dr Rosen's letter was spelt with a capital H.'

Mrs Bantry picked it up.

'So it is,' she said. '*Oh!*'

'Yes, dear,' said Miss Marple. 'I thought you'd notice!'

'There's a definite warning in that letter,' said Colonel Bantry. 'That's the first thing caught my attention. I notice more than you'd think. Yes, a definite warning — against whom?'

'There's rather a curious point about that letter,' said Sir Henry. 'According to Templeton, Dr Rosen opened the letter at breakfast and tossed it across to him saying he didn't know who the fellow was from Adam.'

'But it wasn't a fellow,' said Jane Helier. 'It was signed "Georgina".'

'It's difficult to say which it is,' said Dr Lloyd. 'It might be Georgey; but it certainly looks more like Georgina. Only it strikes me that the writing is a man's.'

'You know, that's interesting,' said Colonel Bantry. 'His tossing it across the table like that and pretending he knew nothing about it. Wanted to watch somebody's face. Whose face – the girl's? or the man's?'

'Or even the cook's?' suggested Mrs Bantry. 'She might have been in the room bringing in the breakfast. But what I don't see is . . . it's most peculiar –'

She frowned over the letter. Miss Marple drew closer to her. Miss Marple's finger went out and touched the sheet of paper. They murmured together.

'But why did the secretary tear up the other letter?' asked Jane Helier suddenly. 'It seems – oh! I don't know – it seems queer. Why should he have letters from Germany? Although, of course, if he's above suspicion, as you say –'

'But Sir Henry didn't say that,' said Miss Marple quickly, looking up from her murmured conference with Mrs Bantry. 'He said *four* suspects. So that shows that he includes Mr Templeton. I'm right, am I not, Sir Henry?'

'Yes, Miss Marple. I have learned one thing through bitter experience. Never say to yourself that *anyone* is above suspicion. I gave you reasons just now why three of these people might after all be guilty, unlikely as it seemed. I did not at that time apply the same process to Charles Templeton. But I came to it at last through pursuing the rule I have just mentioned. And I was forced to recognize this: That every army and every navy and every police force has a certain number of traitors within its ranks, much as we hate to admit the idea. And I examined dispassionately the case against Charles Templeton.

'I asked myself very much the same questions as Miss Helier has just asked. Why should he, alone of all the house, not be able to produce the letter he had received – a letter, moreover, with a German stamp on it. Why should he have letters from Germany?

'The last question was an innocent one, and I actually put it to him. His reply came simply enough. His mother's sister was married to a German. The letter had been from a German girl cousin. So I learned something I did not know before – that Charles Templeton had relations with people in Germany. And that put him definitely on the list of suspects – very much so. He is my own man – a lad I have always liked and trusted; but in common justice and fairness I must admit that he heads that list.

'But there it is – I do not know! I do not *know* . . . And in all probability I never shall know. It is not a question of punishing a murderer. It is a question that to me seems a hundred times more important. It is the blighting, perhaps, of an honourable man's whole career . . . because of suspicion – a suspicion that I dare not disregard.'

Miss Marple coughed and said gently:

'Then, Sir Henry, if I understand you rightly, it is this young Mr Templeton only who is so much on your mind?'

'Yes, in a sense. It should, in theory, be the same for all four, but that is not actually the case. Dobbs, for instance – suspicion may attach to him in my mind, but it will not actually affect his career. Nobody in the village has ever had any idea that old Dr Rosen's death was anything but an accident. Gertrud is slightly more affected. It must make, for instance, a difference in Fräulein Rosen's attitude toward her. But that, possibly, is not of great importance to her.

'As for Greta Rosen – well, here we come to the crux of the matter. Greta is a very pretty girl and Charles

Templeton is a good-looking young man, and for five months they were thrown together with no outer distractions. The inevitable happened. They fell in love with each other – even if they did not come to the point of admitting the fact in words.

'And then the catastrophe happens. It is three months ago now and a day or two after I returned, Greta Rosen came to see me. She had sold the cottage and was returning to Germany, having finally settled up her uncle's affairs. She came to me personally, although she knew I had retired, because it was really about a personal matter she wanted to see me. She beat about the bush a little, but at last it all came out. What did I think? That letter with the German stamp – she had worried about it and worried about it – the one Charles had torn up. Was it all right? Surely it *must* be all right. Of course she believed his story, but – oh! if she only *knew*! If she knew – for certain.

'You see? The same feeling: the wish to trust – but the horrible lurking suspicion, thrust resolutely to the back of the mind, but persisting nevertheless. I spoke to her with absolute frankness, and asked her to do the same. I asked her whether she had been on the point of caring for Charles, and he for her.

'"I think so," she said. "Oh, yes, I know it was so. We were so happy. Every day passed so contentedly. We knew – we both knew. There was no hurry – there was all the time in the world. Some day he would tell me he loved me, and I should tell him that I too – Ah! But you can guess! And now it is all changed. A black cloud has come between us – we are constrained, when we meet we do not know what to say. It is, perhaps, the same with him as with me . . . We are each saying to ourselves, 'If I were *sure*!' That is why, Sir Henry, I beg of you to say to me, 'You may be sure, whoever killed your uncle, it was not Charles Templeton!' Say it to me! Oh, say it to me! I beg – I beg!"

'And, damn it all,' said Sir Henry, bringing down his

fist with a bang on the table, 'I couldn't say it to her. They'll drift farther and farther apart, those two – with suspicion like a ghost between them – a ghost that can't be laid.'

He leant back in his chair, his face looked tired and grey. He shook his head once or twice despondently.

'And there's nothing more can be done, unless –' He sat up straight again and a tiny whimsical smile crossed his face –' unless Miss Marple can help us. Can't you, Miss Marple? I've a feeling that letter might be in your line, you know. The one about the Church Social. Doesn't it remind you of something or someone that makes everything perfectly plain? Can't you do something to help two helpless young people who want to be happy?'

Behind the whimsicality there was something earnest in his appeal. He had come to think very highly of the mental powers of this frail old-fashioned maiden lady. He looked across at her with something very like hope in his eyes.

Miss Marple coughed and smoothed her lace.

'It does remind me a little of Annie Poultny,' she admitted. 'Of course the letter is perfectly plain – both to Mrs Bantry and myself. I don't mean the Church Social letter, but the other one. You living so much in London and not being a gardener, Sir Henry, would not have been likely to notice.'

'Eh?' said Sir Henry. 'Notice what?'

Mrs Bantry reached out a hand and selected a catalogue. She opened it and read aloud with gusto:

'Dr Helmuth Spath. Pure lilac, a wonderfully fine flower, carried on exceptionally long and stiff stem. Splendid for cutting and garden decoration. A novelty of striking beauty.

'Edgar Jackson. Beautifully shaped chrysanthemum-like flower of a distinct brick-red colour.

'Amos Perry. Brilliant red, highly decorative.

'Tsingtau. Brilliant orange-red, showy garden plant and lasting cut flower.

'Honesty –'

'With a capital H, you remember,' murmured Miss Marple.

'Honesty. Rose and white shades, enormous perfect shaped flower.'

Mrs Bantry flung down the catalogue, and said with immense explosive force:

'*Dahlias!*'

'And their initial letters spell "DEATH"', explained Miss Marple.

'But the letter came to Dr Rosen himself,' objected Sir Henry.

'That was the clever part of it,' said Miss Marple. 'That and the warning in it. What would he do, getting a letter from someone he didn't know, full of names he didn't know. Why, of course, toss it over to his secretary.'

'Then, after all –'

'*Oh, no!*' said Miss Marple. '*Not* the secretary. Why, that's what makes it so perfectly clear that it *wasn't* him. He'd never have let that letter be found if so. And equally he'd never have destroyed a letter to himself with a German stamp on it. Really, his innocence is – if you'll allow me to use the word – just *shining*.'

'Then who –'

'Well, it seems almost certain – as certain as anything can be in this world. There was another person at the breakfast table, and she would – quite naturally under the circumstances – put out her hand for the letter and read it. And that would be that. You remember that she got a gardening catalogue by the same post –'

'Greta Rosen,' said Sir Henry, slowly. 'Then her visit to me –'

'Gentlemen never see through these things,' said Miss Marple. 'And I'm afraid they often think we old women are – well, cats, to see things the way we do. But there it is. One does know a great deal about one's own sex, unfortunately. I've no doubt there was a barrier between them. The young man felt a sudden inexplicable repulsion. He suspected, purely through instinct, and couldn't hide the suspicion. And I really think that the girl's visit to you was just pure *spite*. She was safe enough really; but she just went out of her way to fix your suspicions definitely on poor Mr Templeton. You weren't nearly so sure about him until after her visit.'

'I'm sure it was nothing that she said –' began Sir Henry.

'Gentlemen,' said Miss Marple calmly, 'never see through these things.'

'And that girl –' he stopped. 'She commits a cold-blooded murder and gets off Scot free!'

'Oh! no, Sir Henry,' said Miss Marple. 'Not Scot free. Neither you nor I believe that. Remember what you said not long ago. No. Greta Rosen will not escape punishment. To begin with, she must be in with a very queer set of people – blackmailers and terrorists – associates who will do her no good, and will probably bring her to a miserable end. As you say, one mustn't waste thoughts on the guilty – it's the innocent who matter. Mr Templeton, who I daresay will marry that German cousin, his tearing up her letter looks – well, it looks *suspicious* – using the word in quite a different sense from the one we've been using all the evening. A little as though he were afraid of the other girl noticing or asking to see it? Yes, I think there must have been some little romance there. And then there's Dobbs – though, as you say, I daresay it won't matter much to him. His elevenses are probably all he thinks about. And then there's that poor old Gertrud – the one who reminded me of Annie

Poultny. Poor Annie Poultny. Fifty years faithful service and suspected of making away with Miss Lamb's will, though nothing could be proved. Almost broke the poor creature's faithful heart; and then after she was dead it came to light in the secret drawer of the tea caddy where old Miss Lamb had put it herself for safety. But too late then for poor Annie.

'That's what worries me so about that poor old German woman. When one is old, one becomes embittered very easily. I felt much more sorry for her than for Mr Templeton, who is young and good looking and evidently a favourite with the ladies. You will write to her, won't you, Sir Henry, and just tell her that her innocence is established beyond doubt? Her dear old master dead, and she no doubt brooding and feeling herself suspected of . . . Oh! It won't bear thinking about!'

'I will write, Miss Marple,' said Sir Henry. He looked at her curiously. 'You know, I shall never quite understand you. Your outlook is always a different one from what I expect.'

'My outlook, I am afraid, is a very petty one,' said Miss Marple humbly. 'I hardly ever go out of St Mary Mead.'

'And yet you have solved what may be called an International mystery,' said Sir Henry. 'For you *have* solved it. I am convinced of that.'

Miss Marple blushed, then bridled a little.

'I was, I think, well educated for the standard of my day. My sister and I had a German governess – a Fräulein. A very sentimental creature. She taught us the language of flowers – a forgotten study nowadays, but most charming. A yellow tulip, for instance, means Hopeless Love, whilst a China Aster means I die of Jealousy at your feet. That letter was signed Georgine, which I seem to remember is Dahlia in German, and that of course made the whole thing perfectly clear. I wish I could remember the meaning of Dahlia, but alas, that eludes me. My memory is not what it was.'

'At any rate it didn't mean DEATH.'

'No, indeed. Horrible, is it not? There are very sad things in the world.'

'There are,' said Mrs Bantry with a sigh. 'It's lucky one has flowers and one's friends.'

'She puts us last, you observe,' said Dr Lloyd.

'A man used to send me purple orchids every night to the theatre,' said Jane dreamily.

'"I await your favours," – that's what that means,' said Miss Marple brightly.

Sir Henry gave a peculiar sort of cough and turned his head away.

Miss Marple gave a sudden exclamation.

'I've remembered. Dahlias mean "Treachery and Misrepresentation."'

'Wonderful,' said Sir Henry. 'Absolutely wonderful.'

And he sighed.

The Herb of Death

'Now then, Mrs B,' said Sir Henry Clithering encouragingly.

Mrs Bantry, his hostess, looked at him in cold reproof.

'I've told you before that I will *not* be called Mrs B. It's not dignified.'

'Scheherazade, then.'

'And even less am I Sche – what's her name! I never can tell a story properly, ask Arthur if you don't believe me.'

'You're quite good at the facts, Dolly,' said Colonel Bantry, 'but poor at the embroidery.'

'That's just it,' said Mrs Bantry. She flapped the bulb catalogue she was holding on the table in front of her. 'I've been listening to you all and I don't know how you do it. "He said, she said, you wondered, they thought, everyone implied" – well, I just couldn't and there it is! And besides I don't know anything to tell a story about.'

'We can't believe that, Mrs Bantry,' said Dr Lloyd. He shook his grey head in mocking disbelief.

Old Miss Marple said in her gentle voice: 'Surely dear –'

Mrs Bantry continued obstinately to shake her head.

'You don't know how banal my life is. What with the servants and the difficulties of getting scullery maids, and just going to town for clothes, and dentists, and Ascot (which Arthur hates) and then the garden –'

'Ah!' said Dr Lloyd. 'The garden. We all know where your heart lies, Mrs Bantry.'

'It must be nice to have a garden,' said Jane Helier, the beautiful young actress. 'That is, if you hadn't got to dig, or to get your hands messed up. I'm ever so fond of flowers.'

'The garden,' said Sir Henry. 'Can't we take that as a starting point? Come, Mrs B. The poisoned bulb, the deadly daffodils, the herb of death!'

'Now it's odd your saying that,' said Mrs Bantry. 'You've just reminded me. Arthur, do you remember that business at Clodderham Court? You know. Old Sir Ambrose Bercy. Do you remember what a courtly charming old man we thought him?'

'Why, of course. Yes, that *was* a strange business. Go ahead, Dolly.'

'You'd better tell it, dear.'

'Nonsense. Go ahead. Must paddle your own canoe. I did my bit just now.'

Mrs Bantry drew a deep breath. She clasped her hands and her face registered complete mental anguish. She spoke rapidly and fluently.

'Well, there's really not much to tell. The Herb of Death – that's what put it into my head, though in my own mind I call it *sage and onions*.'

'Sage and onions?' asked Dr Lloyd.

Mrs Bantry nodded.

'That was how it happened you see,' she explained. 'We were staying, Arthur and I, with Sir Ambrose Bercy at Clodderham Court, and one day, by mistake (though very stupidly, I've always thought) a lot of foxglove leaves were picked with the sage. The ducks for dinner that night were stuffed with it and everyone was very ill, and one poor girl – Sir Ambrose's ward – died of it.'

She stopped.

'Dear, dear,' said Miss Marple, 'how very tragic.'

'Wasn't it?'

'Well,' said Sir Henry, 'what next?'

'There isn't any next,' said Mrs Bantry, 'that's all.'

Everyone gasped. Though warned beforehand, they had not expected quite such brevity as this.

'But, my dear lady,' remonstrated Sir Henry, 'it can't be all. What you have related is a tragic occurrence, but not in any sense of the word a problem.'

'Well, of course there's some more,' said Mrs Bantry. 'But if I were to tell you it, you'd know what it was.'

She looked defiantly round the assembly and said plaintively:

'I told you I couldn't dress things up and make it sound properly like a story ought to do.'

'Ah ha!' said Sir Henry. He sat up in his chair and adjusted an eyeglass. 'Really, you know, Scheherazade, this is most refreshing. Our ingenuity is challenged. I'm not so sure you haven't done it on purpose – to stimulate our curiosity. A few brisk rounds of "Twenty Questions" is indicated, I think. Miss Marple, will you begin?'

'I'd like to know something about the cook,' said Miss Marple. 'She must have been a very stupid woman, or else very inexperienced.'

'She was just very stupid,' said Mrs Bantry. 'She cried a great deal afterwards and said the leaves had been picked and brought in to her as sage, and how was she to know?'

'Not one who thought for herself,' said Miss Marple. 'Probably an elderly woman and, I daresay, a very good cook?'

'Oh! excellent,' said Mrs Bantry.

'Your turn, Miss Helier,' said Sir Henry.

'Oh! You mean – to ask a question?' there was a pause while Jane pondered. Finally she said helplessly, 'Really – I don't know what to ask.'

Her beautiful eyes looked appealingly at Sir Henry.

'Why not dramatis personae, Miss Helier?' he suggested smiling.

Jane still looked puzzled.

'Characters in order of their appearance,' said Sir Henry gently.

'Oh, yes,' said Jane. 'That's a good idea.'

Mrs Bantry began briskly to tick people off on her fingers.

'Sir Ambrose – Sylvia Keene (that's the girl who died) – a friend of hers who was staying there, Maud Wye, one of those dark ugly girls who manage to make an effort somehow – I never know how they do it. Then there was a Mr Curle who had come down to discuss books with Sir Ambrose – you know, rare books – queer old things in Latin – all musty parchment. There was Jerry Lorimer – he was a kind of next door neighbour. His place, Fairlies, joined Sir Ambrose's estate. And there was Mrs Carpenter, one of those middle-aged pussies who always seem to manage to dig themselves in comfortably somewhere. She was by way of being *dame de compagnie* to Sylvia, I suppose.'

'If it is my turn,' said Sir Henry, 'and I suppose it is, as I'm sitting next to Miss Helier, I want a good deal. I want a short verbal portrait, please, Mrs Bantry, of all the foregoing.'

'Oh!' Mrs Bantry hesitated.

'Sir Ambrose now,' continued Sir Henry. 'Start with him. What was he like?'

'Oh! he was a very distinguished-looking old man – and not so very old really – not more than sixty, I suppose. But he was very delicate – he had a weak heart, could never go upstairs – he had to have a lift put in, and so that made him seem older than he was. Very charming manners – *courtly* – that's the word that describes him best. You never saw him ruffled or upset. He had beautiful white hair and a particularly charming voice.'

'Good,' said Sir Henry. 'I see Sir Ambrose. Now the girl Sylvia – what did you say her name was?'

'Sylvia Keene. She was pretty – really *very* pretty. Fair

haired, you know, and a lovely skin. Not, perhaps, very clever. In fact, rather stupid.'

'Oh! come, Dolly,' protested her husband.

'Arthur, of course, wouldn't think so,' said Mrs Bantry drily. 'But she *was* stupid – she really never said anything worth listening to.'

'One of the most graceful creatures I ever saw,' said Colonel Bantry warmly. 'See her playing tennis – charming, simply charming. And she was full of fun – most amusing little thing. And such a pretty way with her. I bet the young fellows all thought so.'

'That's just where you're wrong,' said Mrs Bantry. 'Youth, as such, has no charms for young men nowadays. It's only old buffers like you, Arthur, who sit maundering on about young girls.'

'Being young's no good,' said Jane. 'You've got to have SA.'

'What,' said Miss Marple, 'is SA?'

'Sex appeal,' said Jane.

'Ah! yes,' said Miss Marple. 'What in my day they used to call "having the come hither in your eye".'

'Not a bad description,' said Sir Henry. 'The *dame de compagnie* you described, I think, as a pussy, Mrs Bantry?'

'I didn't mean a *cat*, you know,' said Mrs Bantry. 'It's quite different. Just a big soft white purry person. Always very sweet. That's what Adelaide Carpenter was like.'

'What sort of aged woman?'

'Oh! I should say fortyish. She'd been there some time – ever since Sylvia was eleven, I believe. A very tactful person. One of those widows left in unfortunate circumstances with plenty of aristocratic relations, but no ready cash. I didn't like her myself – but then I never do like people with very white long hands. And I don't like pussies.'

'Mr Curle?'

'Oh! one of those elderly stooping men. There are so many of them about, you'd hardly know one from the other. He showed enthusiasm when talking about his musty books, but not at any other time. I don't think Sir Ambrose knew him very well.'

'And Jerry next door?'

'A really charming boy. He was engaged to Sylvia. That's what made it so sad.'

'Now I wonder –' began Miss Marple, and then stopped.

'What?'

'Nothing, dear.'

Sir Henry looked at the old lady curiously. Then he said thoughtfully:

'So this young couple were engaged. Had they been engaged long?'

'About a year. Sir Ambrose had opposed the engagement on the plea that Sylvia was too young. But after a year's engagement he had given in and the marriage was to have taken place quite soon.'

'Ah! Had the young lady any property?'

'Next to nothing – a bare hundred or two a year.'

'No rat in that hole, Clithering,' said Colonel Bantry, and laughed.

'It's the doctor's turn to ask a question,' said Sir Henry. 'I stand down.'

'My curiosity is mainly professional,' said Dr Lloyd. 'I should like to know what medical evidence was given at the inquest – that is, if our hostess remembers, or, indeed, if she knows.'

'I know roughly,' said Mrs Bantry. 'It was poisoning by digitalin – is that right?'

Dr Lloyd nodded.

'The active principle of the foxglove – digitalis – acts on the heart. Indeed, it is a very valuable drug in some forms of heart trouble. A very curious case altogther. I would never have believed that eating a preparation of foxglove leaves could possibly result fatally. These ideas of eating poisonous leaves and berries are very much exaggerated. Very few people realize that the vital principle, or alkaloid, has to be extracted with much care and preparation.'

'Mrs MacArthur sent some special bulbs round to Mrs Toomie the other day,' said Miss Marple. 'And Mrs Toomie's cook mistook them for onions, and all the Toomies were very ill indeed.'

'But they didn't die of it,' said Dr Lloyd.

'No. They didn't die of it,' admitted Miss Marple.

'A girl I knew died of ptomaine poisoning,' said Jane Helier.

'We must get on with investigating the crime,' said Sir Henry.

'Crime?' said Jane, startled. 'I thought it was an accident.'

'If it were an accident,' said Sir Henry gently, 'I do not think Mrs Bantry would have told us this story. No, as I read it, this was an accident only in appearance – behind it is something more sinister. I remember a case – various guests in a house party were chatting after dinner. The walls were adorned with all kinds of old-fashioned weapons. Entirely as a joke one of the party seized an ancient horse pistol and pointed it at another man, pretending to fire it. The pistol was loaded and went off, killing the man. We had to ascertain in that case, first, who had secretly prepared and loaded that pistol, and secondly who had so led and directed the conversation that that final bit of horseplay resulted – for the man who had fired the pistol was entirely innocent!

'It seems to me we have much the same problem here. Those digitalin leaves were deliberately mixed with the sage, knowing what the result would be. Since we exonerate the cook – we do exonerate the cook, don't we? – the question arises: Who picked the leaves and delivered them to the kitchen?'

'That's easily answered,' said Mrs Bantry. 'At least the last part of it is. It was Sylvia herself who took the leaves to the kitchen. It was part of her daily job to gather things like salad or herbs, bunches of young carrots – all the sort of things that gardeners never pick right. They hate giving you anything young and tender – they wait for them to be fine specimens. Sylvia and Mrs Carpenter used to see to a lot of these things themselves. And there was foxglove actually growing all amongst the sage in one corner, so the mistake was quite natural.'

'But did Sylvia actually pick them herself?'

'That, nobody ever knew. It was assumed so.'

'Assumptions,' said Sir Henry, 'are dangerous things.'

'But I do know that Mrs Carpenter didn't pick them,' said Mrs Bantry. 'Because, as it happened, she was walking with me on the terrace that morning. We went out there after breakfast. It was unusually nice and warm for early spring. Sylvia went alone down into the garden, but later I saw her walking arm-in-arm with Maud Wye.'

'So they were great friends, were they?' asked Miss Marple.

'Yes,' said Mrs Bantry. She seemed as though about to say something, but did not do so.

'Had she been staying there long?' asked Miss Marple.

'About a fortnight,' said Mrs Bantry.

There was a note of trouble in her voice.

'You didn't like Miss Wye?' suggested Sir Henry.

'I did. That's just it. I did.'

The trouble in her voice had grown to distress.

'You're keeping something back, Mrs Bantry,' said Sir Henry accusingly.

'I wondered just now,' said Miss Marple, 'but I didn't like to go on.'

'When did you wonder?'

'When you said that the young people were engaged. You said that that was what made it so sad. But, if you know what I mean, your voice didn't sound right when you said it – not convincing, you know.'

'What a dreadful person you are,' said Mrs Bantry. 'You always seem to *know*. Yes, I was thinking of something. But I don't really know whether I ought to say it or not.'

'You must say it,' said Sir Henry. 'Whatever your scruples, it mustn't be kept back.'

'Well, it was just this,' said Mrs Bantry. 'One evening – in fact the very evening before the tragedy – I happened to go out on the terrace before dinner. The window in the drawing-room was open. And as it chanced I saw Jerry Lorimer and Maud Wye. He was – well – kissing her. Of course I didn't know whether it was just a sort of chance affair, or whether – well, I mean, one can't *tell*. I knew Sir Ambrose never had really liked Jerry Lorimer – so perhaps he knew he was that kind of young man. But one thing I *am* sure of: that girl, Maud Wye, was *really* fond of him. You'd only to see her looking at him when she was off guard. And I think, too, they were really better suited than he and Sylvia were.'

'I am going to ask a question quickly, before Miss Marple can,' said Sir Henry. 'I want to know whether, after the tragedy, Jerry Lorimer married Maud Wye?'

'Yes,' said Mrs Bantry. 'He did. Six months afterwards.'

'Oh! Scheherezade, Scheherezade,' said Sir Henry. 'To think of the way you told us this story at first! Bare bones indeed – and to think of the amount of flesh we're finding on them now.'

'Don't speak so ghoulishly,' said Mrs Bantry. 'And don't use the word flesh. Vegetarians always do. They say, "I never eat flesh" in a way that puts you right off your little beefsteak. Mr Curle was a vegetarian. He used to eat some peculiar stuff that looked like bran for breakfast. Those elderly stooping men with beards are often faddy. They have patent kinds of underwear, too.'

'What on earth, Dolly,' said her husband, 'do you know about Mr Curle's underwear?'

'Nothing,' said Mrs Bantry with dignity. 'I was just making a guess.'

'I'll amend my former statement,' said Sir Henry. 'I'll say instead that the dramatis personae in your problem are very interesting. I'm beginning to see them all – eh, Miss Marple?'

'Human nature is always interesting, Sir Henry. And it's curious to see how certain types always tend to act in exactly the same way.'

'Two women and a man,' said Sir Henry. 'The old eternal human triangle. Is that the base of our problem here? I rather fancy it is.'

Dr Lloyd cleared his throat.

'I've been thinking,' he said rather diffidently. 'Do you say, Mrs Bantry, that you yourself were ill?'

'Was I not! So was Arthur! So was everyone!'

'That's just it – everyone,' said the doctor. 'You see what I mean? In Sir Henry's story which he told us just now, one man shot another – he didn't have to shoot the whole room full.'

'I don't understand,' said Jane. 'Who shot who?'

'I'm saying that whoever planned this thing went about it very curiously, either with a blind belief in chance, or else with an absolutely reckless disregard for human life. I can hardly believe there is a man capable of deliberately poisoning eight people with the object of removing one amongst them.'

'I see your point,' said Sir Henry, thoughtfully. 'I confess I ought to have thought of that.'

'And mightn't he have poisoned himself too?' asked Jane.

'Was anyone absent from dinner that night?' asked Miss Marple.

Mrs Bantry shook her head.

'Everyone was there.'

'Except Mr Lorimer, I suppose, my dear. He wasn't staying in the house, was he?'

'No; but he was dining there that evening,' said Mrs Bantry.

'Oh!' said Miss Marple in a changed voice. 'That makes all the difference in the world.'

She frowned vexedly to herself.

'I've been very stupid,' she murmured. 'Very stupid indeed.'

'I confess your point worries me, Lloyd,' said Sir Henry.

'How ensure that the girl, and the girl only, should get a fatal dose?'

'You can't,' said the doctor. 'That brings me to the point I'm going to make. *Supposing the girl was not the intended victim after all?*'

'What?'

'In all cases of food poisoning, the result is very uncertain. Several people share a dish. What happens? One or two are slightly ill, two more, say, are seriously indisposed, one dies. That's the way of it – there's no certainty anywhere. But there are cases where another factor might enter in. Digitalin is a drug that acts directly on the heart – as I've told you it's prescribed in certain cases. *Now, there was one person in that house who suffered from a heart complaint.* Suppose he was the victim selected? What would not be fatal to the rest *would* be fatal to him – or so the murderer might reasonably suppose. That the thing turned out differently is only a proof of what I was saying just now – the uncertainty and unreliability of the effects of drugs on human beings.'

'Sir Ambrose,' said Sir Henry, 'you think *he* was the

person aimed at? Yes, yes – and the girl's death was a mistake.'

'Who got his money after he was dead?' asked Jane.

'A very sound question, Miss Helier. One of the first we always ask in my late profession,' said Sir Henry.

'Sir Ambrose had a son,' said Mrs Bantry slowly. 'He had quarrelled with him many years previously. The boy was wild, I believe. Still, it was not in Sir Ambrose's power to disinherit him – Clodderham Court was entailed. Martin Bercy succeeded to the title and estate. There was, however, a good deal of other property that Sir Ambrose could leave as he chose, and that he left to his ward Sylvia. I know this because Sir Ambrose died less than a year after the events I am telling you of, and he had not troubled to make a new will after Sylvia's death. I think the money went to the Crown – or perhaps it was to his son as next of kin – I don't really remember.'

'So it was only to the interest of a son who wasn't there and the girl who died herself to make away with him,' said Sir Henry thoughtfully. 'That doesn't seem very promising.'

'Didn't the other woman get anything?' asked Jane. 'The one Mrs Bantry calls the Pussy woman.'

'She wasn't mentioned in the will,' said Mrs Bantry.

'Miss Marple, you're not listening,' said Sir Henry. 'You're somewhere far away.'

'I was thinking of old Mr Badger, the chemist,' said Miss Marple. 'He had a very young housekeeper – young enough to be not only his daughter, but his grand-daughter. Not a word to anyone, and his family, a lot of nephews and nieces, full of expectations. And when he died, would you believe it, he'd been secretly married to her for two years? Of course Mr Badger was a chemist, and a very rude, common old man as well, and Sir Ambrose Bercy was a very courtly gentleman, so Mrs Bantry says, but for all that human nature is much the same everywhere.'

There was a pause. Sir Henry looked very hard at Miss

Marple who looked back at him with gently quizzical blue eyes. Jane Helier broke the silence.

'Was this Mrs Carpenter good looking?' she asked.

'Yes, in a very quiet way. Nothing startling.'

'She had a very sympathetic voice,' said Colonel Bantry.

'Purring – that's what I call it,' said Mrs Bantry. 'Purring!'

'You'll be called a cat yourself one of these days, Dolly.'

'I like being a cat in my home circle,' said Mrs Bantry. 'I don't much like women anyway, and you know it. I like men and flowers.'

'Excellent taste,' said Sir Henry. 'Especially in putting men first.'

'That was tact,' said Mrs Bantry. 'Well, now, what about my little problem? I've been quite fair, I think. Arthur, don't you think I've been fair?'

'Yes, my dear. I don't think there'll be any inquiry into the running by the stewards of the Jockey Club.'

'First boy,' said Mrs Bantry, pointing a finger at Sir Henry.

'I'm going to be long winded. Because, you see, I haven't really got any feeling of certainty about the matter. First, Sir Ambrose. Well, he wouldn't take such an original method of committing suicide – and on the other hand he certainly had nothing to gain by the death of his ward. Exit Sir Ambrose. Mr Curle. No motive for death of girl. If Sir Ambrose was intended victim, he might possibly have purloined a rare manuscript or two that no one else would miss. Very thin and most unlikely. So I think, that in spite of Mrs Bantry's suspicions as to his underclothing, Mr Curle is cleared. Miss Wye. Motive for death of Sir Ambrose – none. Motive for death of Sylvia pretty strong. She wanted Sylvia's young man, and wanted him rather badly – from Mrs Bantry's account. She was with Sylvia that morning in the garden, so had opportunity to pick leaves. No, we can't dismiss Miss Wye so easily. Young Lorimer. He's got a motive in either case. If he gets rid of his sweetheart, he can marry the other girl. Still it seems a bit drastic to kill her – what's a broken engagement these days? If Sir Ambrose dies, he will marry a rich girl instead of a poor one. That might be important or not – depends on his financial position. If I find that his estate was heavily mortgaged and that Mrs Bantry has deliberately withheld that fact from us, I shall claim a foul. Now Mrs Carpenter. You know, I have suspicions of Mrs Carpenter. Those white hands, for one thing, and her excellent alibi at the time the herbs were picked – I always distrust alibis. And I've got another reason for suspecting her which I will keep to myself. Still, on the whole, if I've got to plump, I shall plump for Miss Maude Wye, because there's more evidence against her than anyone else.'

'Next boy,' said Mrs Bantry, and pointed at Dr Lloyd.

'I think you're wrong, Clithering, in sticking to the theory that the girl's death was meant. I am convinced that the murderer intended to do away with Sir Ambrose. I don't think that young Lorimer had the necessary knowledge. I am inclined to believe that Mrs Carpenter was the guilty party. She had been a long time with the family, knew all about the state of Sir Ambrose's health, and could easily arrange for this girl Sylvia (who, you said yourself, was rather stupid) to pick the right leaves. Motive, I confess, I don't see; but I hazard the guess that Sir Ambrose had at one time made a will in which she was mentioned. That's the best I can do.'

Mrs Bantry's pointing finger went on to Jane Helier.

'I don't know what to say,' said Jane, 'except this: Why shouldn't the girl herself have done it? She took the leaves into the kitchen after all. And you say Sir Ambrose had been sticking out against her marriage. If he died, she'd get the money and be able to marry at once. She'd know just as much about Sir Ambrose's health as Mrs Carpenter would.'

Mrs Bantry's finger came slowly round to Miss Marple. 'Now then, School Marm,' she said.

'Sir Henry has put it all very clearly – very clearly indeed,' said Miss Marple. 'And Dr Lloyd was so right in what he said. Between them they seem to have made things so very clear. Only I don't think Dr Lloyd quite realized one aspect of what he said. You see, not being Sir Ambrose's medical adviser, he couldn't know just what kind of heart trouble Sir Ambrose had, could he?'

'I don't quite see what you mean, Miss Marple,' said Dr Lloyd.

'You're assuming – aren't you? – that Sir Ambrose had the kind of heart that digitalin would affect adversely? But there's nothing to prove that that's so. It might be just the other way about.'

'The other way about?'

'Yes, you did say that it was often prescribed for heart trouble?'

'Even then, Miss Marple, I don't see what that leads to?'

'Well, it would mean that he would have digitalin in his possession quite naturally – without having to account for it. What I am trying to say (I always express myself so badly) is this: Supposing you wanted to poison anyone with a fatal dose of digitalin. Wouldn't the simplest and easiest way be to arrange for everyone to be poisoned – actually by digitalin leaves? It wouldn't be fatal in anyone else's case, of course, but no one would be surprised at one victim because, as Dr Lloyd said, these things are so uncertain. No one would be likely to ask whether the girl had actually had a fatal dose of infusion of digitalis or something of that kind. He might have put it in a cocktail, or in her coffee or even made her drink it quite simply as a tonic.'

'You mean Sir Ambrose poisoned his ward, the charming girl whom he loved?'

'That's just it,' said Miss Marple. 'Like Mr Badger and his young housekeeper. Don't tell me it's absurd for a man of sixty to fall in love with a girl of twenty. It happens every day – and I daresay with an old autocrat like Sir Ambrose, it might take him queerly. These things become a madness sometimes. He couldn't bear the thought of her getting married – did his best to oppose it – and failed. His mad jealousy became so great that he preferred killing her to letting her go to young Lorimer. He must have thought of it some time beforehand, because that foxglove seed would have to be sown among the sage. He'd pick it himself when the time came, and send her into the kitchen with it. It's horrible to think of, but I suppose we must take as merciful a view of it as we can. Gentlemen of that age are sometimes very peculiar indeed where young girls are concerned. Our last organist – but there, I mustn't talk scandal.'

'Mrs Bantry,' said Sir Henry. 'Is this so?'

Mrs Bantry nodded.

'Yes. I'd no idea of it – never dreamed of the thing being anything but an accident. Then, after Sir Ambrose's death, I got a letter. He had left directions to send it to me. He told me the truth in it. I don't know why – but he and I always got on very well together.'

In the momentary silence, she seemed to feel an unspoken criticism and went on hastily:

'You think I'm betraying a confidence – but that isn't so. I've changed all the names. He wasn't really called Sir Ambrose Bercy. Didn't you see how Arthur stared stupidly when I said that name to him? He didn't understand at first. I've changed everything. It's like they say in magazines and in the beginning of books: "All the characters in this story are purely fictitious." You never know who they really are.'

THE MILLION DOLLAR
BOND ROBBERY

'What a number of bond robberies there have been lately!'
I observed one morning, laying aside the newspaper.
'Poirot, let us forsake the science of detection, and take to
crime instead!'

'You are on the – how do you say it? – get-rich-quick
tack, eh, *mon ami*?'

'Well, look at this last *coup*, the million dollars' worth of
Liberty Bonds which the London and Scottish Bank were
sending to New York, and which disappeared in such a
remarkable manner on board the *Olympia*.'

'If it were not for the *mal de mer*, and the difficulty of
practising the so excellent method of Laverguier for a
longer time than the few hours of crossing the Channel, I
should delight to voyage myself on one of these big liners,'
murmured Poirot dreamily.

'Yes, indeed,' I said enthusiastically. 'Some of
them must be perfect palaces; the swimming-baths, the
lounges, the restaurant, the palm courts – really, it must
be hard to believe that one is on the sea.'

'Me, I always know when I am on the sea,' said Poirot
sadly. 'And all those bagatelles that you enumerate, they
say nothing to me: but, my friend, consider for a moment
the geniuses that travel as it were incognito! On board
these floating palaces, as you so justly call them, one
would meet the élite, the *haute noblesse* of the criminal
world!'

I laughed.

'So that's the way your enthusiasm runs! You would

have liked to cross swords with the man who sneaked the Liberty Bonds?'

The landlady interrupted us.

'A young lady as wants to see you, Mr Poirot. Here's her card.'

The card bore the inscription: Miss Esmée Farquhar, and Poirot, after diving under the table to retrieve a stray crumb, and putting it carefully in the waste-paper basket, nodded to the landlady to admit her.

In another minute one of the most charming girls I have ever seen was ushered into the room. She was perhaps about five-and-twenty, with big brown eyes and a perfect figure. She was well-dressed and perfectly composed in manner.

'Sit down, I beg of you, mademoiselle. This is my friend, Captain Hastings, who aids me in my little problems.'

'I am afraid it is a big problem I have brought you today, Monsieur Poirot,' said the girl, giving me a pleasant bow as she seated herself. 'I dare say you have read about it in the papers. I am referring to the theft of Liberty Bonds on the *Olympia*.' Some astonishment must have shown itself on Poirot's face, for she continued quickly: 'You are doubtless asking yourself what have I to do with a grave institution like the London and Scottish Bank. In one sense nothing, in another sense everything. You see, Monsieur Poirot, I am engaged to Mr Philip Ridgeway.'

'Aha! and Mr Philip Ridgeway – '

'Was in charge of the bonds when they were stolen. Of course no actual blame can attach to him, it was not his fault in any way. Nevertheless, he is half distraught over the matter, and his uncle, I know, insists that he must carelessly have mentioned having them in his possession. It is a terrible set-back to his career.'

'Who is his uncle?'

'Mr Vavasour, joint general manager of the London and Scottish Bank.'

'Suppose, Miss Farquhar, that you recount to me the whole story?'

'Very well. As you know, the Bank wished to extend their credits in America, and for this purpose decided to send over a million dollars in Liberty bonds. Mr Vavasour selected his nephew, who had occupied a position of trust in the Bank for many years and who was conversant with all the details of the Bank's dealings in New York, to make the trip. The *Olympia* sailed from Liverpool on the 23rd, and the bonds were handed over to Philip on the morning of that day by Mr Vavasour and Mr Shaw, the two joint general managers of the London aand Scottish Bank. They were counted, enclosed in a package, and sealed in his presence, and he then locked the package at once in his portmanteau.'

'A portmanteau with an ordinary lock?'

'No, Mr Shaw insisted on a special lock being fitted to it by Hubbs. Philip, as I say, placed the package at the bottom of the trunk. It was stolen just a few hours before reaching New York. A rigorous search of the whole ship was made, but without result. The bonds seemed literally to have vanished into thin air.'

Poirot made a grimace.

'But they did not vanish absolutely, since I gather that they were sold in small parcels within half an hour of the docking of the *Olympia*! Well, undoubtedly the next thing is for me to see Mr Ridgeway.'

'I was about to suggest that you should lunch with me at the "Cheshire Cheese". Philip will be there. He is meeting me, but does not yet know that I have been consulting you on his behalf.'

We agreed to this suggestion readily enough, and drove there in a taxi.

Mr Philip Ridgeway was there before us, and looked somewhat surprised to see his fiancée arriving with two complete strangers. He was a nice-looking young fellow, tall and spruce, with a touch of greying hair at the temples, though he could not have been much over thirty.

Miss Farquhar went up to him and laid her hand on his arm.

'You must forgive me acting without consulting you, Philip,' she said. 'Let me introduce you to Monsieur Hercule Poirot, of whom you must often have heard, and his friend, Captain Hastings.'

Ridgeway looked very astonished.

'Of course I have heard of you, Monsieur Poirot,' he said, as he shook hands. 'But I had no idea that Esmée was thinking of consulting you about my – our trouble.'

'I was afraid you would not let me do it, Philip,' said Miss Farquhar meekly.

'So you took care to be on the safe side,' he observed, with a smile. 'I hope Monsieur Poirot will be able to throw some light on this extraordinary puzzle, for I confess frankly that I am nearly out of my mind with worry and anxiety about it.'

Indeed, his face looked drawn and haggard and showed only too clearly the strain under which he was labouring.

'Well, well,' said Poirot. 'Let us lunch, and over lunch we will put our heads together and see what can be done. I want to hear Mr Ridgeway's story from his own lips.'

Whilst we discussed the excellent steak and kidney pudding of the establishment, Philip Ridgeway narrated the circumstances leading to the disappearance of the bonds. His story agreed with that of Miss Farquhar in every particular. When he had finished, Poirot took up the thread with a question.

'What exactly led you to discover that the bonds had been stolen, Mr Ridgeway?'

He laughed rather bitterly.

'The thing stared me in the face, Monsieur Poirot. I couldn't have missed it. My cabin trunk was half out from under the bunk and all scratched and cut about where they'd tried to force the lock.'

'But I understood that it had been opened with a key?'

'That's so. They tried to force it, but couldn't. And in the end, they must have got it unlocked somehow or other.'

'Curious,' said Poirot, his eyes beginning to flicker with the green light I knew so well. 'Very curious! They waste much, much time trying to prise it open, and then – *sapristi!* they find they have the key all the time – for each of Hubbs's locks are unique.'

'That's just why they couldn't have had the key. It never left me day or night.'

'You are sure of that?'

'I can swear to it, and besides, if they had had the key or a duplicate, why should they waste time trying to force an obviously unforceable lock?'

'Ah! there is exactly the question we are asking ourselves! I venture to prophesy that the solution, if we ever find it, will hinge on that curious fact. I beg of you not to assault me if I ask you one more question: *Are you perfectly certain that you did not leave the trunk unlocked?*'

Philip Ridgeway merely looked at him, and Poirot gesticulated apologetically.

'Ah, but these things can happen, I assure you! Very well, the bonds were stolen from the trunk. What did the thief do with them? How did he manage to get ashore with them?'

'Ah!' cried Ridgeway. 'That's just it. How? Word was passed to the Customs authorities, and every soul that left the ship was gone over with a toothcomb!'

'And the bonds, I gather, made a bulky package?'

'Certainly they did. They could hardly have been hidden on board – and anyway we know they weren't, because they were offered for sale within half an hour of the *Olympia*'s arrival, long before I got the cables going and the numbers sent out. One broker swears he bought some of them even before the *Olympia* got in. But you can't send bonds by wireless.'

'Not by wireless, but did any tug come alongside?'

'Only the official ones, and that was after the alarm was given when everyone was on the look-out. I was watching out myself for their being passed over to someone that way. My God, Monsieur Poirot, this thing will drive me mad! People are beginning to say I stole them myself.'

'But you also were searched on landing, weren't you?' asked Poirot gently.

'Yes.'

The young man stared at him in a puzzled manner.

'You do not catch my meaning, I see,' said Poirot, smiling enigmatically. 'Now I should like to make a few inquiries at the Bank.'

Ridgeway produced a card and scribbled a few words on it.

'Send this in and my uncle will see you at once.'

Poirot thanked him, bade farewell to Miss Farquhar, and together we started out for Threadneedle Street and the head office of the London and Scottish Bank. On production of Ridgeway's card, we were led through the labyrinth of counters and desks, skirting paying-in clerks and paying-out clerks and up to a small office on the first floor where the joint general managers received us. They were two grave gentlemen, who had grown grey in the service of the Bank. Mr Vavasour had a short white beard, Mr Shaw was clean shaven.

'I understand you are strictly a private inquiry agent?' said Mr Vavasour. 'Quite so, quite so. We have, of course, placed ourselves in the hands of Scotland Yard. Inspector McNeil has charge of the case. A very able officer, I believe.'

'I am sure of it,' said Poirot politely. 'You will permit a

few questions, on your nephew's behalf? About this lock, who ordered it from Hubbs's?'

'I ordered it myself,' said Mr Shaw. 'I would not trust to any clerk in the matter. As to the keys, Mr Ridgeway had one, and the other two are held by my colleague and myself.'

'And no clerk has had access to them?'

Mr Shaw turned inquiringly to Mr Vavasour.

'I think I am correct in saying that they have remained in the safe where we placed them on the 23rd,' said Mr Vavasour. 'My colleague was unfortunately taken ill a fortnight ago – in fact on the very day that Philip left us. He has only just recovered.'

'Severe bronchitis is no joke to a man of my age,' said Mr Shaw ruefully. 'But I'm afraid Mr Vavasour has suffered from the hard work entailed by my absence, especially with this unexpected worry coming on top of everything.'

Poirot asked a few more questions. I judged that he was endeavouring to gauge the exact amount of intimacy between uncle and nephew. Mr Vavasour's answers were brief and punctilious. His nephew was a trusted official of the Bank, and had no debts or money difficulties that he knew of. He had been entrusted with similar missions in the past. Finally we were politely bowed out.

'I am disappointed,' said Poirot, as we emerged into the street.

'You hoped to discover more? They are such stodgy old men.'

'It is not their stodginess which disappoints me, *mon ami*. I do not expect to find a Bank manager a "keen financier with an eagle glance", as your favourite works of fiction put it. No, I am disappointed in the case – it is too easy!'

'*Easy?*'

'Yes, do you not find it almost childishly simple?'

'You know who stole the bonds?'

'I do.'

'But then – we must – why –'

'Do not confuse and fluster yourself, Hastings. We are not going to do anything at present.'

'But why? What are you waiting for?'

'For the *Olympia*. She is due on her return trip from New York on Tuesday.'

'But if you know who stole the bonds, why wait? He may escape.'

'To a South Sea island where there is no extradition? No, *mon ami*, he would find life very uncongenial there. As to why I wait – *eh bien*, to the intelligence of Hercule Poirot the case is perfectly clear, but for the benefit of others, not so greatly gifted by the good God – the Inspector, McNeil, for instance – it would be as well to make a few inquiries to establish the facts. One must have consideration for those less gifted than oneself.'

'Good Lord, Poirot! Do you know, I'd give a considerable sum of money to see you make a thorough ass of yourself – just for once. You're so confoundedly conceited!'

'Do not enrage yourself, Hastings. In verity, I observe that there are times when you almost detest me! Alas, I suffer the penalties of greatness.'

The little man puffed out his chest, and sighed so comically that I was forced to laugh.

Tuesday saw us speeding to Liverpool in a first-class carriage of the L & NWR. Poirot had obstinately refused to enlighten me as to his suspicions – or certainties. He contented himself with expressing surprise that I, too, was not equally *au fait* with the situation. I disdained to argue, and entrenched my curiosity behind a rampart of pretended indifference.

Once arrived at the quay alongside which lay the big transatlantic liner, Poirot became brisk and alert. Our proceedings consisted in interviewing four successive stewards and inquiring after a friend of Poirot's who had crossed to New York on the 23rd.

'An elderly gentleman, wearing glasses. A great invalid, hardly moved out of his cabin.'

The description appeared to tally with one Mr Ventnor who had occupied the cabin C 24 which was next to that of Philip Ridgeway. Although unable to see how Poirot had deduced Mr Ventnor's existence and personal appearance, I was keenly excited.

'Tell me,' I cried, 'was this gentleman one of the first to land when you got to New York?'

The steward shook his head.

'No, indeed, sir, he was one of the last off the boat.'

I retired crestfallen, and observed Poirot grinning at me. He thanked the steward, a note changed hands, and we took our departure,

'It's all very well,' I remarked heatedly, 'but that last answer must have damned your precious theory, grin as you please!'

'As usual, you see nothing, Hastings. That last answer is, on the contrary, the coping-stone of my theory.'

I flung up my hands in despair.

'I give it up.'

When we were in the train, speeding towards London, Poirot wrote busily for a few minutes, sealing up the result in an envelope.

'This is for the good Inspector McNeil. We will leave it at Scotland Yard in passing, and then to the Rendezvous Restaurant, where I have asked Miss Esmée Farquhar to do us the honour of dining with us.'

'What about Ridgeway?'

'What about him?' asked Poirot with a twinkle.

'Why, you surely don't think – you can't –'

'The habit of incoherence is growing upon you,

Hastings. As a matter of fact I *did* think. If Ridgeway had been the thief -- which was perfectly possible -- the case would have been charming; a piece of neat methodical work.'

'But not so charming for Miss Farquhar.'

'Possibly you are right. Therefore all is for the best. Now, Hastings, let us review the case. I can see that you are dying to do so. The sealed package is removed from the trunk and vanishes, as Miss Farquhar puts it, into thin air. We will dismiss the thin air theory, which is not practicable at the present stage of science, and consider what is likely to have become of it. Everyone asserts the incredulity of its being smuggled ashore --'

'Yes, but we know --'

'*You* may know, Hastings, I do not. I take the view that, since it seemed incredible, it *was* incredible. Two possibilities remain: it was hidden on board -- also rather difficult -- or it was thrown overboard.'

'With a cork on it, do you mean?'

'Without a cork.'

I stared.

'But if the bonds were thrown overboard, they couldn't have been sold in New York.'

'I admire your logical mind, Hastings. The bonds were sold in New York, therefore they were not thrown overboard. You see where that leads us?'

'Where we were when we started.'

'*Jamais de la vie!* If the package was thrown overboard, and the bonds were sold in New York, the package could not have contained the bonds. Is there any evidence that the package *did* contain the bonds? Remember, Mr Ridgeway never opened it from the time it was placed in his hands in London.'

'Yes, but then --'

Poirot waved an impatient hand.

'Permit me to continue. The last moment that the bonds

are seen as bonds is in the office of the London and Scottish Bank on the morning of the 23rd. They reappear in New York half an hour after the *Olympia* gets in, and according to one man, whom nobody listens to, actually *before* she gets in. Supposing then, that they have never been on the Olympia at all? Is there any other way they could get to New York? Yes. The *Gigantic* leaves Southampton on the same day as the *Olympia*, and she holds the record for the Atlantic. Mailed by the *Gigantic*, the bonds would be in New York the day before the *Olympia* arrived. All is clear, the case begins to explain itself. The sealed packet is only a dummy, and the moment of its substitution must be in the office in the bank. It would be an easy matter for any of the three men present to have prepared a duplicate package which could be substituted for the genuine one. *Très bien*, the bonds are mailed to a confederate in New York, with instructions to sell as soon as the *Olympia* is in, but someone must travel on the *Olympia* to engineer the supposed moment of robbery.'

'But why?'

'Because if Ridgeway merely opens the packet and finds it a dummy, suspicion flies at once to London. No, the man on board in the cabin next door does his work, pretends to force the lock in an obvious manner so as to draw immediate attention to the theft, really unlocks the trunk with a duplicate key, throws the package overboard and waits until the last to leave the boat. Naturally he wears glasses to conceal his eyes, and is an invalid since he does not want to run the risk of meeting Ridgeway. He steps ashore in New York and returns by the first boat available.'

'But who – which was he?'

'The man who had a duplicate key, the man who ordered the lock, the man who has *not* been severely ill with bronchitis at his home in the country – *enfin*, the "stodgy" old man, Mr Shaw! There are criminals in high places sometimes, my friend. Ah, here we are. Mademoiselle, I have succeeded! You permit?'

And, beaming, Poirot kissed the astonished girl lightly on either cheek!

THE TRAGEDY AT MARSDON MANOR

I had been called away from town for a few days, and on my return found Poirot in the act of strapping up his small valise.

'*A le bonne heure*, Hastings, I feared you would not have returned in time to accompany me.'

'You are called away on a case, then?'

'Yes, though I am bound to admit that, on the face of it, the affair does not seem promising. The Northern Union Insurance Company have asked me to investigate the death of a Mr Maltravers who a few weeks ago insured his life with them for the large sum of fifty thousand pounds.'

'Yes?' I said, much interested.

'There was, of course, the usual suicide clause in the policy. In the event of his committing suicide within a year the premiums would be forfeited. Mr Maltravers was duly examined by the Company's own doctor, and although he was a man slightly past the prime of life was passed as being in quite sound health. However, on Wednesday last – the day before yesterday – the body of Mr Maltravers was found in the grounds of his house in Essex, Marsdon Manor, and the cause of his death is described as some kind of internal haemorrhage. That in itself would be nothing remarkable, but sinister rumours as to Mr Maltravers' financial position have been in the air of late, and the Northern Union have ascertained beyond any possible doubt that the deceased gentleman stood upon the verge of bankruptcy. Now that alters matters considerably. Maltravers had a beautiful young wife, and it is suggested that he got together all the ready money he could for the purpose of paying the premiums on a life insurance for his wife's benefit, and then committed suicide. Such a thing is not uncommon. In any case, my friend Alfred Wright, who is a director of the Northern Union, has asked me to investigate the facts of the case, but, as I told him, I am not very hopeful of success. If the cause of death had been heart failure, I should have been more sanguine. Heart failure may always be translated as the inability of the local GP to discover what his patient really did die of, but a haemorrhage seems fairly definite. Still, we can but make some necessary inquiries. Five minutes to pack your bag, Hastings, and we will take a taxi to Liverpool Street.'

About an hour later, we alighted from a Great Eastern train at the little station of Marsdon Leigh. Inquiries at the station yielded the information that Marsdon Manor was about a mile distant. Poirot decided to walk, and we betook ourselves along the main street.

'What is our plan of campaign?' I asked.

'First I will call upon the doctor. I have ascertained that there is only one doctor in Marsdon Leigh, Dr Ralph Bernard. Ah, here we are at his house.'

The house in question was a kind of superior cottage, standing back a little from the road. A brass plate on the gate bore the doctor's name. We passed up the path and rang the bell.

We proved to be fortunate in our call. It was the doctor's consulting hour, and for the moment there were no patients waiting for him. Dr Bernard was an elderly man, high-shouldered and stooping, with a pleasant vagueness of manner.

Poirot introduced himself and explained the purpose of our visit, adding that Insurance Companies were bound to investigate fully in a case of this kind.

'Of course, of course,' said Dr Bernard vaguely. 'I

suppose, as he was such a rich man, his life was insured for a big sum?'

'You consider him a rich man, doctor?'

The doctor looked rather surprised.

'Was he not? He kept two cars, you know, and Marsdon Manor is a pretty big place to keep up, although I believe he bought it very cheap.'

'I understand that he had had considerable losses of late,' said Poirot, watching the doctor narrowly.

The latter, however, merely shook his head sadly.

'Is that so? Indeed. It is fortunate for his wife, then, that there is this life insurance. A very beautiful and charming young creature, but terribly unstrung by this sad catastrophe. A mass of nerves, poor thing. I have tried to spare her all I can, but of course the shock was bound to be considerable.'

'You had been attending Mr Maltravers recently?'

'My dear sir, I never attended him.'

'What?'

'I understand Mr Maltravers was a Christian Scientist — or something of that kind.'

'But you examined the body?'

'Certainly. I was fetched by one of the under-gardeners.'

'And the cause of death was clear?'

'Absolutely. There was blood on the lips, but most of the bleeding must have been internal.'

'Was he still lying where he had been found?'

'Yes, the body had not been touched. He was lying at the edge of a small plantation. He had evidently been out shooting rooks, a small rook rifle lay beside him. The haemorrhage must have occurred quite suddenly. Gastric ulcer, without a doubt.'

'No question of his having been shot, eh?'

'My dear sir!'

'I demand pardon,' said Poirot humbly. 'But, if my

memory is not at fault, in the case of a recent murder, the doctor first gave a verdict of heart failure – altering it when the local constable pointed out that there was a bullet wound through the head!'

'You will not find any bullet wounds on the body of Mr Maltravers,' said Dr Bernard dryly. 'Now gentlemen, if there is nothing further – '

We took the hint.

'Good morning, and many thanks to you, doctor, for so kindly answering our questions. By the way, you saw no need for an autopsy?'

'Certainly not.' The doctor became quite apoplectic. 'The cause of death was clear, and in my profession we see no need to distress unduly the relatives of a dead patient.'

And turning, the doctor slammed the door sharply in our faces.

'And what do you think of Dr Bernard, Hastings?' inquired Poirot, as we proceeded on our way to the Manor.

'Rather an old ass.'

'Exactly. Your judgements of character are always profound, my friend.'

I glanced at him uneasily, but he seemed perfectly serious. A twinkle, however, came into his eye, and he added slyly:

'That is to say, where there is no question of a beautiful woman!'

I looked at him coldly.

On our arrival at the manor-house, the door was opened to us by a middle-aged parlourmaid. Poirot handed her his card, and a letter from the Insurance Company for Mrs Maltravers. She showed us into a small morning-room, and retired to tell her mistress. About ten minutes elapsed, and then the door opened, and a slender figure in widow's weeds stood upon the threshold.

'Monsieur Poirot?' she faltered.

'Madame!' Poirot sprang gallantly to his feet and hastened towards her. 'I cannot tell you how I regret to derange you in this way. But what will you? *Les affaires* – they know no mercy.'

Mrs Maltravers permitted him to lead her to a chair. Her eyes were red with weeping, but the temporary disfigurement could not conceal her extraordinary beauty. She was about twenty-seven or eight, and very fair, with large blue eyes and a pretty pouting mouth.

'It is something about my husband's insurance, is it? But must I be bothered *now* – so soon?'

'Courage, my dear madame. Courage! You see, your late husband insured his life for rather a large sum, and in such a case the Company always has to satisfy itself as to a few details. They have emppowered me to act for them. You can rest assured that I will do all in my power to render the matter not too unpleasant for you. Will you recount to me briefly the sad events of Wednesday?'

'I was changing for tea when my maid came up – one of the gardeners had just run to the house. He had found – '

Her voice trailed away. Poirot pressed her hand sympathetically.

'I comprehend. Enough! You had seen your husband earlier in the afternoon?'

'Not since lunch. I had walked down to the village for some stamps, and I believe he was out pottering round the grounds.'

'Shooting rooks, eh?'

'Yes, he usually took his little rook rifle with him, and I heard one or two shots in the distance.'

'Where is this little rook rifle now?'

'In the hall, I think.'

She led the way out of the room and found and handed the little weapon to Poirot, who examined it cursorily.

'Two shots fired, I see,' he observed, as he handed it back. 'And now, madame, if I might see – '

He paused delicately.

'The servant shall take you,' she murmured, averting her head.

The parlourmaid, summoned, led Poirot upstairs. I remained with the lovely and unfortunate woman. It was hard to know whether to speak or remain silent. I essayed one or two general reflections to which she responded absently, and in a very few minutes Poirot rejoined us.

'I thank you for all your courtesy, madame. I do not think you need be troubled any further with this matter. By the way, do you know anything of your husband's financial position?'

She shook her head.

'Nothing whatever. I am very stupid over business things.'

'I see. Then you can give us no clue as to why he suddenly decided to insure his life? He had not done so previously, I understand.'

'Well, we had only been married a little over a year. But, as to why he insured his life, it was because he had absolutely made up his mind that he would not live long. He had a strong premonition of his own death. I gather that he had had one haemorrhage already, and that he knew that another one would prove fatal. I tried to dispel these gloomy fears of his, but without avail. Alas, he was only too right!'

Tears in her eyes, she bade us a dignified farewell. Poirot made a characteristic gesture as we walked down the drive together.

'*Eh bien*, that is that! Back to London, my friend, there appears to be no mouse in this mouse-hole. And yet – '

'Yet what?'

'A slight discrepancy, that is all! You noticed it? You did not? Still, life is full of discrepancies, and assuredly the man cannot have taken his life – there is no poison that would fill his mouth with blood. No, no, I must resign myself to the fact that all here is clear and above-board – but who is this?'

A tall young man was striding up the drive towards us. He passed us without making any sign, but I noted that he was not ill-looking, with a lean, deeply-bronzed face that spoke of life in a tropic clime. A gardener who was sweeping up leaves had paused for a minute in his task, and Poirot ran quickly up to him.

'Tell me, I pray you, who is that gentleman? Do you know him?'

'I don't remember his name, sir, though I did hear it. He was staying down here last week for a night. Tuesday, it was.'

'Quick, *mon ami*, let us follow him.'

We hastened up the drive after the retreating figure. A glimpse of a black-robed figure on the terrace at the side of the house, and our quarry swerved and we after him, so that we were witnesses of the meeting.

Mrs Maltravers almost staggered where she stood, and her face blanched noticeably.

'You,' she gasped. 'I thought you were on the sea – on your way to East Africa?'

'I got some news from my lawyers that detained me,' explained the young man. 'My old uncle in Scotland died unexpectedly and left me some money. Under the circumstances I thought it better to cancel my passage. Then I saw this bad news in the paper and I came down to see if there was anything I could do. You'll want someone to look after things for you a bit perhaps.'

At that moment they became aware of our presence. Poirot stepped forward, and with many apologies explained that he had left this stick in the hall. Rather reluctantly, it seemed to me, Mrs Maltravers made the necessary introduction.

'Monsieur Poirot, Captain Black.'

A few minutes' chat ensued, in the course of which

Poirot elicited the fact that Captain Black was putting up at the Anchor Inn. The missing stick not having been discovered (which was not surprising), Poirot uttered more apologies and we withdrew.

We returned to the village at a great pace, and Poirot made a bee line for the Anchor Inn.

'Here we establish ourselves until our friend the Captain returns,' he explained. 'You noticed that I emphasized the point that we were returning to London by the first train? Possibly you thought I meant it. But no – you observed Mrs Maltravers' face when she caught sight of this young Black? She was clearly taken aback, and he – *eh bien*, he was very devoted, did you not think so? And he was here on Tuesday night – the day before Mr Maltravers died. We must investigate the doings of Captain Black, Hastings.'

In about half an hour we espied our quarry approaching the inn. Poirot went out and accosted him and presently brought him up to the room we had engaged.

'I have been telling Captain Black of the mission which brings us here,' he explained. 'You can understand, *monsieur le capitaine*, that I am anxious to arrive at Mr Maltravers' state of mind immediately before his death, and that at the same time I do not wish to distress Mrs Maltravers unduly by asking her painful questions. Now, you were here just before the occurrence, and can give us equally valuable information.'

'I'll do anything I can to help you, I'm sure,' replied the young soldier, 'but I'm afraid I didn't notice anything out of the ordinary. You see, although Maltravers was an old friend of my people's, I didn't know him very well myself.'

'You came down – when?'

'Tuesday afternoon. I went up to town early Wednesday morning, as my boat sailed from Tilbury about twelve o'clock. But some news I got made me alter my plans, as I dare say you heard me explain to Mrs Maltravers.'

'You were returning to East Africa, I understand.'

'Yes. I've been out there ever since the War – a great country.'

'Exactly. Now what was the talk about at dinner on Tuesday night?'

'Oh, I don't know. The usual odd topics. Maltravers asked after my people, and then we discussed the question of German reparations, and then Mrs Maltravers asked a lot of questions about East Africa, and I told them one or two yarns, that's about all, I think.'

'Thank you.'

Poirot was silent for a moment, then he said gently: 'With your permission, I should like to try a little experiment. You have told us all that your conscious self knows, I want now to question your subconscious self.'

'Psycho-analysis, what?' said Black, with visible alarm.

'Oh, no,' said Poirot reassuringly. 'You see, it is like this, I give you a word, you answer with another, and so on. Any word, the first you think of. Shall we begin?

'All right,' said Black slowly, but he looked uneasy.

'Note down the words, please, Hastings,' said Poirot. Then he took from his pocket his big turnip-faced watch and laid it on the table beside him. 'We will commence. Day.'

There was a moment's pause, and then Black replied: '*Night.*'

As Poirot proceeded, his answers came quicker.

'Name,' said Poirot.

'*Place.*'

'Bernard.'

'*Shaw.*'

'Tuesday.'

'*Dinner.*'

'Journey.'

'*Ship.*'

'Country.'
'*Uganda.*'
'Story.'
'*Lions.*'
'Rook Rifle.'
'*Farm.*'
'Shot.'
'*Suicide.*'
'Elephant.'
'*Tusks.*'
'Money.'
'*Lawyers.*'

'Thank you, Captain Black. Perhaps you could spare me a few minutes in about half an hour's time?'

'Certainly.' The young soldier looked at him curiously and wiped his brow as he got up.

'And now, Hastings,' said Poirot, smiling at me as the door closed behind him. 'You see it all, do you not?'

'I don't know what you mean.'

'Does that list of words tell you nothing?'

I scrutinized it, but was forced to shake my head.

'I will assist you. To begin with, Black answered well within the normal time limit, with no pauses, so we can take it that he himself has no guilty knowledge to conceal. "Day" to "Night" and "Place" to "Name" are normal associations. I began work with "Bernard", which might have suggested the local doctor had he come across him at all. Evidently he had not. After our recent conversation, he gave "Dinner" to my "Tuesday", but "Journey" and "Country" were answered by "Ship" and "Uganda", showing clearly that it was his journey abroad that was important to him and not the one which brought him down here. "Story" recalls to him one of the "Lion" stories he told at dinner. I proceeded to "Rook Rifle" and he answered with the totally unexpected word "Farm".

When I say "Shot", he answers at once "Suicide". The association seems clear. A man he knows committed suicide with a rook rifle on a farm somewhere. Remember, too, that his mind is still on the stories he told at dinner, and I think you will agree that I shall not be far from the truth if I recall Captain Black and ask him to repeat the particular suicide story which he told at the dinner-table on Tuesday evening.'

Black was straightforward enough over the matter.

'Yes, I did tell them that story now that I come to think of it. Chap shot himself on a farm out there. Did it with a rook rifle through the roof of the mouth, bullet lodged in the brain. Doctors were no end puzzled over it – there was nothing to show except a little blood on the lips. But what – ?'

'What has it got to do with Mr Maltravers? You did not know, I see, that he was found with a rook rifle by his side.'

'You mean my story suggested to him – oh, but that is awful!'

'Do not distress yourself – it would have been one way or another. Well, I must get on the telephone to London.'

Poirot had a lengthy conversation over the wire, and came back thoughtful. He went off by himself in the afternoon, and it was not till seven o'clock that he announced that he could put it off no longer, but must break the news to the young widow. My sympathy had already gone out to her unreservedly. To be left penniless, and with the knowledge that her husband had killed himself to assure her future was a hard burden for any woman to bear. I cherished a secret hope, however, that young Black might prove capable of consoling her after her first grief had passed. He evidently admired her enormously.

Our interview with the lady was painful. She refused vehemently to believe the facts that Poirot advanced, and when she was at last convinced broke down into bitter weeping. An examination of the body turned our suspicions into certainty. Poirot was very sorry for the poor lady, but, after all, he was employed by the Insurance Company, and what could he do? As he was preparing to leave he said gently to Mrs Maltravers:

'Madame, you of all people should know that there are no dead!'

'What do you mean?' she faltered, her eyes growing wide.

'Have you never taken part in any spiritualistic séances? You are mediumistic, you know.'

'I have been told so. But you do not believe in Spiritualism, surely?'

'Madam, I have seen some strange things. You know that they say in the village that this house is haunted?'

She nodded, and at that moment the parlourmaid announced that dinner was ready.

'Won't you just stay and have something to eat?'

We accepted gracefully, and I felt that our presence could not but help distract her a little from her own griefs.

We had just finished our soup, when there was a scream outside the door, and the sound of breaking crockery. We jumped up. The parlourmaid appeared, her hand to her heart.

'It was a man – standing in the passage.'

Poirot rushed out, returning quickly.

'There is no one there.'

'Isn't there, sir?' said the parlourmaid weakly. 'Oh it did give me a start!'

'But why?'

She dropped her voice to a whisper.

'I thought – I thought it was the master – it looked like 'im.'

I saw Mrs Maltravers give a terrified start, and my mind flew to the old superstition that a suicide cannot rest. She thought of it too, I am sure, for a minute later, she caught Poirot's arm with a scream.

'Didn't you hear that? Those three taps on the window? That's how *he* always used to tap when he passed round the house.'

'The ivy,' I cried. 'It was the ivy against the pane.'

But a sort of terror was gaining on us all. The parlourmaid was obviously unstrung, and when the meal was over Mrs Maltravers besought Poirot not to go at once. She was clearly terrified to be left alone. We sat in the little morning-room. The wind was getting up, and moaning round the house in an eerie fashion. Twice the door of the room came unlatched and the door slowly opened, and each time she clung to me with a terrified gasp.

'Ah, but this door, it is bewitched!' cried Poirot angrily, at last. He got up and shut it once more, then turned the key in the lock. 'I shall lock it, so!'

'Don't do that,' she gasped. 'If it should come open now – '

And even as she spoke the impossible happened. The locked door slowly swung open. I could not see into the passage from where I sat, but she and Poirot were facing it. She gave one long shriek as she turned to him.

'You saw him – there in the passage?' she cried.

He was staring down at her with a puzzled face, then shook his head.

'I saw him – my husband – you must have seen him too?'

'Madame, I saw nothing. You are not well – unstrung – '

'I am perfectly well, I – Oh, God!'

Suddenly without warning, the lights quivered and went out. Out of the darkness came three loud raps. I could hear Mrs Maltravers moaning.

And then – I saw!

The man I had seen on the bed upstairs stood there facing us, gleaming with a faint ghostly light. There was blood on his lips, and he held his right hand out, pointing. Suddenly a brilliant light seemed to proceed from it. It passed over Poirot and me, and fell on Mrs Maltravers. I saw her white terrified face, and something else!

'My God, Poirot!' I cried. 'Look at her hand, her right hand. It's all red!'

Her own eyes fell on it, and she collapsed in a heap on the floor.

'Blood,' she cried hysterically. 'Yes, it's blood. I killed him. I did it. He was showing me, and then I put my hand on the trigger and pressed. Save me from him – save me! He's come back!'

Her voice died away in a gurgle.

'Lights,' said Poirot briskly.

The lights went on as if by magic.

'That's it,' he continued. 'You heard, Hastings? And you, Everett? Oh, by the way, this is Mr Everett, rather a fine member of the theatrical profession. I phoned to him this afternoon. His make-up is good, isn't it? Quite like the dead man, and with a pocket torch and the necessary phosphorescence he made the proper impression. I shouldn't touch her right hand if I were you, Hastings. Red paint marks so. When the lights went out I clasped her hand, you see. By the way, we mustn't miss our train. Inspector Japp is outside the window. A bad night – but he has been able to while away the time by tapping on the window every now and then.

'You see,' continued Poirot, as we walked briskly through the wind and rain, 'there was a little discrepancy. The doctor seemed to think the deceased was a Christian Scientist, and who could have given him that impression but Mrs Maltravers? But to us she represented him as being in a great state of apprehension about his own health. Again, why was she so taken aback by the reappearance of young Black? And lastly although I know that convention decrees that a woman must make a decent pretence of mourning for her husband, I do not care for such heavily-rouged eyelids! You did not observe them, Hastings? No? As I always tell you, you see nothing!

'Well, there it was. There were the two possibilities. Did Black's story suggest an ingenious method of committing suicide to Mr Maltravers, or did his other listener, the wife, see an equally ingenious method of committing murder? I inclined to the latter view. To shoot himself in the way indicated, he would probably have had to pull the trigger with his toe – or at least so I imagine. Now if Maltravers had been found with one boot off, we should almost certainly have heard of it from someone. An odd detail like that would have been remembered.

'No, as I say, I inclined to the view that it was a case of murder, not suicide, but I realized that I had not a shadow of proof in support of my theory. Hence the elaborate little comedy you saw played tonight.'

'Even now I don't quite see all the details of the crime,' I said.

'Let us start from the beginning. Here is a shrewd and scheming woman who, knowing of her husband's financial *débâcle* and tired of the elderly mate she has only married for his money, induces him to insure his life for a large sum, and then seeks for the means to accomplish her purpose. An accident gives her that – the young soldier's strange story. The next afternoon when *monsieur le capitaine*, as she thinks, is on the high seas, she and her husband are strolling round the grounds. "What a curious story that was last night!" she observes. "Could a man shoot himself in such a way? Do show me if it is possible!" The poor fool – he shows her. He places the end of his rifle in his mouth. She stoops down, and puts her finger on the trigger, laughing up at him. "And now, sir," she says saucily. "Supposing I pull the trigger?"

'And then – and then, Hastings – she pulls it!'

THE MYSTERY OF HUNTER'S LODGE

'After all,' murmured Poirot. 'it is possible that I shall not die this time.'

Coming from a convalescent influenza patient, I hailed the remark as showing a beneficial optimism. I myself had been the first sufferer from the disease. Poirot in his turn had gone down. He was now sitting up in bed, propped up with pillows, his head muffled in a woollen shawl, and was slowly sipping a particularly noxious *tisane* which I had prepared according to his directions. His eye rested with pleasure upon a neatly graduated row of medicine bottles which adorned the mantelpiece.

'Yes, yes,' my little friend continued. 'Once more shall I be myself again, the great Hercule Poirot, the terror of evil-doers! Figure to yourself, *mon ami*, that I have a little paragraph to myself in *Society Gossip*. But yes! Here it is: "Go it – criminals – all out! Hercule Poirot – and believe me, girls, he's some Hercules! – our own pet society detective can't get a grip on you. 'Cause why? 'Cause he's got *la grippe* himself"!'

I laughed.

'Good for you, Poirot. You are becoming quite a public character. And fortunately you haven't missed anything of particular interest during this time.'

'That is true. The few cases I have had to decline did not fill me with any regret.'

Our landlady stuck her head in at the door.

'There's a gentleman downstairs. Says he must see Monsieur Poirot or you, Captain. Seeing as he was in a great to-do – and with all that quite the gentleman – I brought up 'is card.'

She handed me a bit of pasteboard. 'Mr Roger Havering,' I read.

Poirot motioned with his head towards the bookcase, and I obediently pulled forth *Who's Who*. Poirot took it from me and scanned the pages rapidly.

'Second son of fifth Baron Windsor. Married 1913 Zoe, fourth daughter of William Crabb.'

'H'm!' I said. 'I rather fancy that's the girl who used to act at the Frivolity – only she called herself Zoe Carrisbrook. I remember she married some young man about town just before the War.'

'Would it interest you, Hastings, to go down and hear what our visitor's particular little trouble is? Make him all my excuses.'

Roger Havering was a man of about forty, well set up and of smart appearance. His face, however, was haggard and he was evidently labouring under great agitation.

'Captain Hastings? You are Monsieur Poirot's partner, I understand. It is imperative that he should come with me to Derbyshire today.'

'I'm afraid that's impossible,' I replied. 'Poirot is ill in bed – influenza.'

His face fell.

'Dear me, that is a great blow to me.'

'The matter on which you want to consult him is serious?'

'My God, yes! My uncle, the best friend I have in the world, was foully murdered last night.'

'Here in London?'

'No, in Derbyshire. I was in town and received a telegram from my wife this morning. Immediately upon its receipt I determined to come round and beg Monsieur Poirot to undertake the case.'

'If you will excuse me a minute,' I said, struck by a sudden idea.

I rushed upstairs, and in a few brief words acquainted

Poirot with the situation. He took any further words out of my mouth.

'I see. I see. You want to go yourself, is it not so? Well, why not? You should know my methods by now. All I ask is that you should report to me fully every day, and follow implicitly any instructions I may wire you.'

To this I willingly agreed.

An hour later I was sitting opposite Mr Havering in a first-class carriage on the Midland Railway, speeding rapidly away from London.

'To begin with, Captain Hastings, you must understand that Hunter's Lodge, where we are going, and where the tragedy took place, is only a small shooting-box in the heart of the Derbyshire moors. Our real home is near Newmarket, and we usually rent a flat in town for the season. Hunter's Lodge is looked after by a housekeeper who is quite capable of doing all we need when we run down for an occasional week-end. Of course, during the shooting season, we take down some of our own servants from Newmarket. My uncle, Mr Harrington Pace (as you may know, my mother was a Miss Pace of New York), has, for the last three years, made his home with us. He never got on well with my father, or my elder brother, and I suspect that my being somewhat of a prodigal son myself rather increased than diminished his affection towards me. Of course I am a poor man, and my uncle was a rich one – in other words, he paid the piper! But, though exacting in many ways, he was not really hard to get on with, and we all three lived very harmoniously together. Two days ago, my uncle, rather wearied with some recent gaieties of ours in town, suggested that we should run down to Derbyshire for a day or two. My wife telegraphed to Mrs Middleton, the housekeeper, and we went down that same afternoon. Yesterday evening I was forced to return to town, but my wife and my uncle remained on. This morning I received this telegram,' He handed it over to me:

> 'Come at once uncle Harrington murdered last night
> bring good detective if you can but do come – Zoe.'

'Then, as yet you know no details?'

'No, I suppose it will be in the evening papers. Without doubt the police are in charge.'

It was about three o'clock when we arrived at the little station of Elmer's Dale. From there a five-mile drive brought us to a small grey stone building in the midst of the rugged moors.

'A lonely place,' I observed with a shiver.

Havering nodded.

'I shall try and get rid of it. I could never live here again.'

We unlatched the gate and were walking up the narrow path to the oak door when a familiar figure emerged and came to meet us.

'Japp!' I ejaculated.

The Scotland Yard inspector grinned at me in a friendly fashion before addressing my companion.

'Mr Havering, I think? I've been sent down from London to take charge of this case, and I'd like a word with you, if I may, sir.'

'My wife –'

'I've seen your good lady, sir – and the housekeeper. I won't keep you a moment, but I am anxious to get back to the village now that I've seen all there is to see here.'

'I know nothing as yet as to what –'

'Ex-actly,' said Japp soothingly. 'But there are just one or two little points I'd like your opinion about all the same. Captain Hastings here, he knows me, and he'll go on up to the house and tell them you're coming. What have you done with the little man, by the way, Captain Hastings?'

'He's ill in bed with influenza.'

'Is he now? I'm sorry to hear that. Rather the case of the cart without the horse, you being here without him, isn't it?'

And on his rather ill-timed jest I went on to the house. I rang the bell, as Japp had closed the door behind him. After some moments it was opened to me by a middle-aged woman in black.

'Mr Havering will be here in a moment,' I explained. 'He has been detained by the inspector. I have come down with him from London to look into the case. Perhaps you can tell me briefly what occurred last night.'

'Come inside, sir.' She closed the door behind me, and we stood in the dimly-lighted hall. 'It was after dinner last night, sir, that the man came. He asked to see Mr Pace, sir, and, seeing that he spoke the same way, I thought it was an American gentleman friend of Mr Pace's and I showed him into the gun-room, and then went to tell Mr Pace. He wouldn't give any name, which, of course, was a bit odd, now I come to think of it. I told Mr Pace, and he seemed puzzled like, but he said to the mistress: "Excuse me, Zoe, while I see what this fellow wants." He went off to the gun-room, and I went back to the kitchen, but after a while I heard loud voices, as if they were quarrelling, and I came out into the hall. At the same time, the mistress she comes out too, and just then there was a shot and then a dreadful silence. We both ran to the gun-room door, but it was locked and we had to go round to the window. It was open, and there inside was Mr Pace, all shot and bleeding.'

'What became of the man?'

'He must have got away through the window, sir, before we got to it.'

'And then?'

'Mrs Havering sent me to fetch the police. Five miles to walk it was. They came back with me, and the constable he stayed all night, and this morning the police gentleman from London arrived.'

'What was this man like who called to see Mr Pace?'

The housekeeper reflected.

'He had a black beard, sir, and was about middle-aged,

and had on a light overcoat. Beyond the fact that he spoke like an American I didn't notice much about him.'

'I see. Now I wonder if I can see Mrs Havering?'

'She's upstairs, sir. Shall I tell her?'

'If you please. Tell her that Mr Havering is outside with Inspector Japp, and that the gentleman he has brought back with him from London is anxious to speak to her as soon as possible.'

'Very good, sir.'

I was in a fever of impatience to get all the facts. Japp had two or three hours' start on me, and his anxiety to be gone made me keen to be close at his heels.

Mrs Havering did not keep me waiting long. In a few minutes I heard a light step descending the stairs, and looked up to see a very handsome young woman coming towards me. She wore a flame-coloured jumper, that set off the slender boyishness of her figure. On her dark head was a little hat of flame-coloured leather. Even the present tragedy could not dim the vitality of her personality.

I introduced myself, and she nodded in quick comprehension.

'Of course I have often heard of you and your colleague, Monsieur Poirot. You have done some wonderful things together, haven't you? It was very clever of my husband to get you so promptly. Now will you ask me questions? That is the easiest way, isn't it, of getting to know all you want to about this dreadful affair?'

'Thank you, Mrs Havering. Now what time was it that this man arrived?'

'It must have been just before nine o'clock. We had finished dinner, and were sitting over our coffee and cigarettes.'

'Your husband had already left for London?'

'Yes, he went up by the 6.15.'

'Did he go by car to the station, or did he walk?'

'Our own car isn't down here. One came out from the

garage in Elmer's Dale to fetch him in time for the train.'

'Was Mr Pace quite his usual self?'

'Absolutely. Most normal in every way.'

'Now, can you describe this visitor at all?'

'I'm afraid not. I didn't see him. Mrs Middleton showed him straight into the gun-room and then came to tell my uncle.'

'What did your uncle say?'

'He seemed rather annoyed, but went off at once. It was about five minutes later that I heard the sound of raised voices. I ran out into the hall and almost collided with Mrs Middleton. Then we heard the shot. The gun-room door was locked on the inside, and we had to go right round the house to the window. Of course that took some time, and the murderer had been able to get well away. My poor uncle' – her voice faltered – 'had been shot through the head. I saw at once that he was dead. I sent Mrs Middleton for the police, I was careful to touch nothing in the room but to leave it exactly as I found it.'

I nodded approval.

'Now, as to the weapon?'

'Well, I can make a guess at it, Captain Hastings. A pair of revolvers of my husband's were mounted upon the wall. One of them is missing. I pointed this out to the police, and they took the other one away with them. When they have extracted the bullet, I suppose they will know for certain.'

'May I go to the gun-room?'

'Certainly. The police have finished with it. But the body has been removed.'

She accompanied me to the scene of the crime. At that moment Havering entered the hall, and with a quick apology his wife ran to him. I was left to undertake my investigations alone.

I may as well confess at once that they were rather disappointing. In detective novels clues abound, but here I could find nothing that struck me as out of the ordinary except a large blood-stain on the carpet where I judged the dead man had fallen. I examined everything with painstaking care and took a couple of pictures of the room with my little camera which I had brought with me. I also examined the ground outside the window, but it appeared to have been so heavily trampled that I judged it was useless to waste time over it. No, I had seen all that Hunter's Lodge had to show me. I must go back to Elmer's Dale and get into touch with Japp. Accordingly I took leave of the Haverings, and was driven off in the car that had brought us from the station.

I found Japp at the Matlock Arms and he took me forthwith to see the body. Harrington Pace was a small, spare, clean-shaven man, typically American in appearance. He had been shot through the back of the head, and the revolver had been discharged at close quarters.

'Turned away for a moment,' remarked Japp, 'and the other fellow snatched up a revolver and shot him. The one Mrs Havering handed over to us was fully loaded and I suppose the other one was also. Curious what darn fool things people do. Fancy keeping two loaded revolvers hanging up on your wall.'

'What do you think of the case?' I asked, as we left the gruesome chamber behind us.

'Well, I'd got my eye on Havering to begin with. Oh, yes!' – noting my exclamation of astonishment. 'Havering has one or two shady incidents in his past. When he was a boy at Oxford there was some funny business about the signature on one of his father's cheques. All hushed up of course. Then, he's pretty heavily in debt now, and they're the kind of debts he wouldn't like to go to his uncle about, whereas you may be sure the uncle's will would be in his favour. Yes, I'd got my eye on him, and that's why I wanted to speak to him before he saw his wife, but their statements dovetail all right, and I've been to the station and there's no doubt whatever that he left by the 6.15.

That gets up to London about 10.30. He went straight to his club, he says, and if that's confirmed all right – why, he couldn't have been shooting his uncle here at nine o'clock in a black beard!'

'Ah, yes, I was going to ask you what you thought about that beard?'

Japp winked.

'I think it grew pretty fast – grew in the five miles from Elmer's Dale to Hunter's Lodge. Americans that I've met are mostly clean-shaven. Yes, it's amongst Mr Pace's American associates that we'll have to look for the murderer. I questioned the housekeeper first, and then her mistress, and their stories agree all right, but I'm sorry Mrs Havering didn't get a look at the fellow. She's a smart woman, and she might have noticed something that would set us on the track.'

I sat down and wrote a minute and lengthy account to Poirot. I was able to add various further items of information before I posted the letter.

The bullet had been extracted and was proved to have been fired from a revolver identical with the one held by the police. Furthermore, Mr Havering's movements on the night in question had been checked and verified, and it was proved beyond doubt that he had actually arrived in London by the train in question. And, thirdly a sensational development had occurred. A city gentleman, living at Ealing, on crossing Haven Green to get to the District Railway Station that morning, had observed a brown-paper parcel stuck between the railings. Opening it, he found that it contained a revolver, He handed the parcel over to the local police station, and before night it was proved to be the one we were in search of, the fellow to that given us by Mrs Havering. One bullet had been fired from it.

All this I added to my report. A wire from Poirot arrived whilst I was at breakfast the following morning:

'Of course black-bearded man was not Havering only you or Japp would have such an idea wire me description of housekeeper and what clothes she wore this morning same of Mrs Havering do not waste time taking photographs of interiors they are under-exposed and not in the least artistic.'

It seemed to me that Poirot's style was unnecessarily facetious. I also fancied he was a shade jealous of my position on the spot with full facilities for handling the case. His request for a description of the clothes worn by the two women appeared to me to be simply ridiculous, but I complied as well as I, a mere man, was able to.

At eleven a reply wire came from Poirot:

'Advise Japp arrest housekeeper before it is too late.'

Dumbfounded, I took the wire to Japp. He swore softly under his breath.

'He's the goods, Monsieur Poirot: if he says so, there's something in it. And I hardly noticed the woman. I don't know that I can go so far as arresting her, but I'll have her watched. We'll go up right away, and take another look at her.'

But it was too late. Mrs Middleton, that quiet middle-aged woman, who had appeared so normal and respectable, had vanished into thin air. Her box had been left behind. It contained only ordinary wearing apparel. There was no clue to her identity, or as to her whereabouts.

From Mrs Havering we elicited all the facts we could:

'I engaged her about three weeks ago when Mrs Emery, our former housekeeper, left. She came to me from Mrs Selbourne's Agency in Mount Street – a very well-known place. I get all my servants from there. They sent several women to see me, but this Mrs Middleton seemed much the nicest, and had splendid references. I engaged her on the spot, and notified the Agency of the fact. I can't believe that there was anything wrong with her. She was such a nice quiet woman.'

The thing was certainly a mystery. Whilst it was clear that the woman herself could not have committed the crime, since at the moment the shot was fired Mrs Havering was with her in the hall, nevertheless she must have some connection with the murder, or why should she suddenly take to her heels and bolt?

I wired the latest development to Poirot and suggested returning to London and making inquiries at Selbourne's Agency.

Poirot's reply was prompt:

'Useless to inquire at agency they will never have heard of her find out what vehicle took her up to hunters lodge when she first arrived there.'

Though mystified, I was obedient. The means of transport in Elmer's Dale were limited. The local garage had two battered Ford cars, and there were two station flies. None of these had been requisitioned on the date in question. Questioned, Mrs Havering explained that she had given the woman the money for her fare down to Derbyshire and sufficient to hire a car or fly to take her up to Hunter's Lodge. There was usually one of the Fords at the station on the chance of its being required. Taking into consideration the further fact that nobody at the station had noticed the arrival of a stranger, black-bearded or otherwise, on the fatal evening, everything seemed to point to the conclusions that the murderer had come to the spot in a car, which had been waiting near at hand to aid his escape, and that the same car had brought the mysterious housekeeper to her new post. I may mention that inquiries at the Agency in London bore out Poirot's prognostication. No such woman as 'Mrs Middleton' had ever been on their books. They had received the Hon. Mrs Havering's application for a housekeeper, and had sent her various applicants for the post. When she sent them the engagement fee, she omitted to mention which woman she had selected.

Somewhat crestfallen, I returned to London. I found Poirot established in an armchair by the fire in a garish, silk dressing gown. He greeted me with much affection.

'*Mon ami* Hastings! But how glad I am to see you. Veritably I have for you a great affection! And you have enjoyed yourself? You have run to and fro with the good Japp? You have interrogated and investigated to your heart's content?'

'Poirot,' I cried, 'the thing's a dark mystery! It will never be solved.'

'It is true that we are not likely to cover ourselves with glory over it.'

'No, indeed. It's a hard nut to crack.'

'Oh, as far as that goes, I am very good at cracking the nuts! A veritable squirrel! It is not that which embarrasses me. I know well enough who killed Mr Harrington Pace.'

'You know? How did you find out?'

'Your illuminating answers to my wires supplied me with the truth. See here, Hastings let us examine the facts methodically and in order. Mr Harrington Pace is a man with a considerable fortune which at his death will doubtless pass to his nephew. Point No. 1. His nephew is known to be desperately hard up. Point No. 2. His nephew is also known to be — shall we say a man of rather loose moral fibre? Point No. 3.'

'But Roger Havering is proved to have journeyed straight up to London.'

'*Précisément* — and therefore, as Mr Havering left Elmer's Dale at 6.15, and since Mr Pace cannot have been killed before he left, or the doctor would have spotted the time of the crime as being given wrongly when he examined the body, we conclude quite rightly, that Mr Havering did *not* shoot his uncle. But there is a Mrs Havering, Hastings.'

'Impossible! The housekeeper was with her when the shot was fired.'

'Ah, yes, the housekeeper. But she has disappeared.'

'She will be found.'

'I think not. There is something peculiarly elusive about that housekeeper, don't you think so, Hastings? It struck me at once.'

'She played her part, I suppose, and then got out in the nick of time.'

'And what was her part?'

'Well, presumably to admit her confederate, the black-bearded man.'

'Oh, no, that was not her part! Her part was what you have just mentioned, to provide an alibi for Mrs Havering at the moment the shot was fired. And no one will ever find her, *mon ami*, because she does not exist! "There's no such person," as your so great Shakespeare says.'

'It was Dickens,' I murmured, unable to suppress a smile. 'But what do you mean, Poirot?'

'I mean that Zoe Havering was an actress before her marriage, that you and Japp only saw the housekeeper in a dark hall, a dim middle-aged figure in black with a faint subdued voice, and finally that neither you nor Japp, nor the local police whom the housekeeper fetched, ever saw Mrs Middleton and her mistress at one and the same time. It was child's play for that clever and daring woman. On the pretext of summoning her mistress, she runs upstairs, slips on a bright jumper and a hat with black curls attached which she jams down over the grey transformation. A few deft touches, and the make-up is removed, a slight dusting of rouge, and the brilliant Zoe Havering comes down with her clear ringing voice. Nobody looks particularly at the housekeeper. Why should they? There is nothing to connect her with the crime. She, too, has an alibi.'

'But the revolver that was found at Ealing? Mrs Havering could not have placed it there?'

'No, that was Roger Havering's job – but it was a mistake on their part. It put me on the right track. A man who has committed murder with a revolver which he found on the spot would fling it away at once, he would not carry it up to London with him. No, the motive was clear, the criminals wished to focus the interest of the police on a spot far removed from Derbyshire, they were anxious to get the police away as soon as possible from the vicinity of Hunter's Lodge. Of course the revolver found at Ealing was not the one with which Mr Pace was shot. Roger Havering discharged one shot from it, brought it up to London, went straight to his club to establish his alibi, then went quickly out to Ealing by the District, a matter of about twenty minutes only, placed the parcel where it was found and so back to town. That charming creature, his wife, quietly shoots Mr Pace after dinner – you remember he was shot from behind? Another significant point, that! – reloads the revolver and puts it back in its place, and then starts off with her desperate little comedy.'

'It's incredible,' I muttered, fascinated, 'and yet – '

'And yet it is true. *Bien sûr*, my friend, it is true. But to bring that precious pair to justice, that is another matter. Well, Japp must do what he can – I have written him fully – but I very much fear, Hastings, that we shall be obliged to leave them to Fate, or *le bon Dieu*, whichever you prefer.'

'The wicked flourish like a green bay tree,' I reminded him.

'But at a price, Hastings, always at a price, *croyez-moi!*'

Poirot's forebodings were confirmed. Japp, though convinced of the truth of his theory, was unable to get together the necessary evidence to ensure a conviction.

Mr Pace's huge fortune passed into the hands of his murderers. Nevertheless, Nemesis did overtake them, and when I read in the paper that the Hon. Roger and Mrs Havering were amongst those killed in the crashing of the Air Mail to Paris I knew that Justice was satisfied.

If you have enjoyed this book you may be interested to know about the Agatha Christie Society.

The Society was formed in March 1993 to promote communication between the many loyal fans of Agatha Christie and the various media who strive to bring her works to the public.

The Agatha Christie Society is run under the auspices of Agatha Christie Limited, so we can guarantee that all the information you receive through the Society has been gathered by those people who have a commitment to and love of Agatha Christie.

Members receive four newsletters a year, each one packed with information about Agatha Christie. There are interviews with the personalities who have brought Agatha Christie's characters to life on the stage and screen; behind-the-scenes aspects of filming; publishing worldwide; listings of where you can see productions of Agatha Christie plays and much, much more.

These newsletters are very much a two-way operation, and many of the articles are written by members from around the world.

Meetings are arranged from time to time to give members the opportunity to gather together and exchange information about their favourite writer.

If you would like to become a member, please write to:

The Agatha Christie Society
PO Box 985
London SW1X 9XA